Murder In
Key West
1

Edited by
Shirrel Rhoades

Habent Sua Fata Libelli

ABSOLUTELY AMAZING eBOOKS

Manhanset House
Shelter Island Hts., New York 11965-0342

bricktower@aol.com • tech@absolutelyamazingebooks.com
• absolutelyamazingebooks.com

Library of Congress Cataloging-in-Publication Data
Rhoades, Shirrel, editor
Murder In Key West 1
p. cm.
1. Fiction / Thrillers / Suspense. 2. Fiction / Mystery & Detective / Collections & Anthologies. 3. Fiction / Thrillers / Crime. Fiction, I. Title.
ISBN: 978-1-955036-68-9, Trade Paper

December 2023

Murder In Key West 1

Murder and Mayhem In Paradise

Edited by

Shirrel Rhoades

The pen is mightier than the sword, they say.
But what about weapons ranging from flare guns to spear guns to a coconut?
You'll find them all in this murderous anthology.

Here's to those who plot such murders –
mystery writers!

Introduction

About The Authors

Introduction

The name Key West is based in murder. Rather than a designation for a westerly island, it's a vocal translation of the original Spanish name, Cayo Hueso. This literally means Island of Bones. That's because the early discoverers found the island littered with mounds of bones left over from battles between warring Indian tribes. Murder from the very beginning of the island's history.

So to collect stories about murder in Key West into this volume seems very natural. This end-of-the-road town has had a turbulent past – pirates and wreckers, thieves and bubbas. At one time it was the richest per capita town in the United States. At another, the poorest. With economic swings like that, you can count on a few murders.

The murders herein are all fictional. And all in fun.

Key West has long been known as a haven for writers – from Ernest Hemingway to Robert Stone, Tennessee Williams to Thomas McGuane, Robert Frost to John Ciardi, Shel Silverstein to Annie Dillard. Mystery writers, too.

We have collected a sampling from some of the leading mystery writers living and working in Key West today. And who write about Key West as if it were the hero of the piece.

-Shirrel Rhoades
Key West

So curl up, lock the door, pull down the shades, and enjoy a good murder mystery set in an island paradise.

- Shirrel Rhoades
Key West

1. Murder in Key West

Michael Haskins

Tony Whyte's once sparking blue eyes were lifeless and stared into oblivion; his frozen expression suggested no fear or pain, not even surprise and his Key West tan had turned ashen. Both hands clutched an old sword blade that had been forced through his chest and impaled him to the boat chair where he died. A small pirate flag hung from its handle.

A puddle of congealed blood sloshed like Jell-O under the chair as the luxurious 50-foot trawler rocked in its slip. The teak-paneled main cabin appeared neat, only Tony looked out of place, while the sweet stickiness of blood, mixed with the sourness of death fouled the cabin's air.

I searched for a pulse in his neck, but knew I wouldn't find one. Tony was as cold as granite from a Quincy quarry and almost as hard.

Classical music played from the trawler's satellite radio. I looked at the radio's screen and *Bach, cello suite no. 6 in D major by Pablo Casals* scrolled across it. The music was counterpoint to the cacophony of sounds coming from the Key West Old Town marina outside Schooner Wharf Bar; a mixture of bar patrons' happiness, captains barking orders to crews, tourists shrieking excitement, boat engines revving and traffic.

I walked outside to breath the salty air. Too many people had seen me on the boat, so I couldn't walk away. Not that I wanted to. Tony was a guy I had worked with years ago on a newspaper in Puerto Rico. We had taken different roads in life, but two months ago, our paths crossed again in Key West, Florida, my home.

Tony had been sober four years and was writing again. He was happy and talked freely of his alcoholism, of waking confused and scared from his blackouts, and how long it had taken him to hit bottom. His journalism career crashed and burned, while mine flourished. Slowly and sober, Tony had been writing his way back, one day at a time.

I looked inside the cabin and thought again about how neat it was. Tony had been a barfly, a scraper who knew how to survive, but this time he hadn't. He knew who killed him, but hadn't seen it coming.

I sat in a deck chair and felt the morning sun on my face. Clouds moved across the pale sky and the air smelled of saltwater, humidity and seaweed. Tarpon broke the surface, their splashing echoed around the marina. It smelled a lot better than inside. Lines, holding boats in place, moaned from stress and birds cried in protest, as the first reef bound catamarans, filled with tourists waiting to sunburn, left for a day of snorkeling.

The sounds of life vibrated from the marina and harbor walk, while the silence of murder sat quietly in the boat's cabin.

I used my cell phone to call Richard Dowley, the chief of police. Had someone, or something from Tony's alcohol-hazy past found him? Or, had a murderer with a pirate fetish surfaced in Paradise? Murder was almost unheard of in Key West. We were more than 100 miles from Miami and a million miles from its violence.

~~~

The Chief, dressed in creased blue slacks and a blue Polo shirt with a police logo on its breast, stood with a Styrofoam cup of *café con leche*, a mixture of strong Cuban coffee with hot milk and lots of sugar, sunglasses perched on his large nose, looking at Tony's body.

Sherlock Corcoran, the crime scene investigator, and Detective Luis Morales, both wearing surgical gloves, looked cautiously around the room. They had turned the boat's air condition to high, but the room still held the stench of violent death. Few new Sherlock's real first name, but the nickname came with his job.

Their casual attire conflicted with my cutoff jeans, sleeveless button-downed collared shirt, faded pre-World Series Boston Red Sox baseball cap and flip-flops. I had three good cigars in my pocket and wanted to light one, to help kill the foul air.

"Who was he?" the Chief sipped his *con leche*. "And how do you know him?"

"Tony Whyte," I turned away and looked outside. "Whyte with a Y. Years ago we worked on the same paper in San Juan."

"What's he doing on Wizard's boat?"

"He was helping Wizard and his two partners write their memoirs on discovering the Spanish treasure." It was the truth, but not the whole truth.

When I mentioned the Spanish treasure, Sherlock and Luis stopped and stared at me. The three boat bums – Wizard, Lucky and Bubba – discovering millions in Spanish treasure in the '70s was a Key West legend with little, if any truth told with the story. When the new multi millionaires were sober they had varying stories about the discovery and they told other versions when they were drunk, which was often. Their only consistency was their inconsistency.

"Wizard do this?" the Chief took a long swallow and finished his *con leche*.

"No, I don't think so."

"Why?" He took a cigar from my pocked, sniffed it, and smiled.

"Wizard's too frail and this guy is twice his size," Luis said. "He didn't do it. Whoever did it had enough strength to push the sword through a man's ribs."

The Chief looked at me and I nodded. Wizard was in his late 70s and had always been a beanpole. In his prime, he had a difficulty with a scuba tank until he was in the water.

"Let's talk to him anyway," he said to Luis and handed the cigar back. "Have a car check the bars," he looked at his watch. "There are only a few open this early."

Luis went outside to tell the uniformed officers.

"Awfully neat for a murder," Sherlock opened a cabinet and looked inside. "This the way you found it, Mick?"

"Exactly. I checked Tony for a pulse and then called the Chief."

"You couldn't tell he was dead?" Sherlock tried to hide a smile. "I'm going below."

Sherlock walked the narrow steps to the lower section of the trawler.

"You want to tell me anything?" the Chief put his empty cup down. "If he's writing the memoir, what are you doing here?"

"He was supposed get with Wizard at the Breakfast Club at Schooner Wharf. Tony said they had a few things to discuss and then he wanted to talk to me." I turned back toward Tony and wondered what he wanted. "We were gonna meet at Schooner and go have breakfast, when he didn't show up I walked down here and found him like this."

"Maybe Wizard had help," the Chief thought aloud.

"No fuss, no mess," I looked around the neat cabin and wished I was outside. "A patrol car is looking for him, Chief," Luis walked in.

"Sherlock's down below," the Chief said and Luis went in search of him.

"What are you going to do now?"

"Go have breakfast at Harpoon Harry's."

"This doesn't bother you?" He seemed surprised.

"Chief, I've covered drug wars, gang wars, revolutions, and riots in L.A., and I've learned to be grateful it ain't my blood on the streets, and appreciate I'm still alive and capable of being hungry."

"You'll need to come to the station and give Luis a statement," the Chief said as I headed toward the deck.

"You know the guy hates me."

"Yeah, but I love you," he smiled. "Come to the station when he calls."

"Sure." I walked outside, took a deep breath, and fought the urge to look at Tony one last time.

~~~

Padre Thomas Collins sat at one of Schooner Wharf's empty thatched-roof patio tables drinking a *con leche* and eating an egg sandwich on Cuban bread. He wore dark cargo shorts, a faded blue dress shirt, the sleeves rolled up past his elbows, with an opened package of Camel cigarettes in the pocket, and sandals.

He motioned me over and pointed to a second Styrofoam cup. I picked it up and was surprised to find it warm.

"For me?"

"I thought you might want it," he looked up and smiled. "What do you think happened?"

Padre Thomas, as he liked to be called, grew up Irish Catholic outside of Boston. He became a missionary priest, had a parish church in Guatemala and about ten years ago walked away from his rectory. For the past eight years, he has been in Key West. Rumor is he lives on a stipend from the Church, but rumors run rampant around the island and rarely hold any grains of truth. His skin is tanned like leather from riding his bike, his only mode of transportation. He volunteers at a hospice and the Catholic soup kitchen, otherwise his time is his own.

I met Padre Thomas at Schooner Wharf a few months after he first arrived and everyone warned me that he was crazy, because he claimed to see and talk to angels. I believe he sees the angels, but I haven't made up my mind on whether or not he's crazy. He still considers himself a priest, but without a church.

"It's not Wizard," I sat down and took the lid off the *con leche*.

"I know," he bit into his sandwich. "I think they'll find him having breakfast at Harpoon's."

"Wizard?"

"Yes, I saw him outside there as I left."

"The angels tell you anything about this?" I sipped from the Styrofoam cup.

He looked up with a devilish grin. "Someone is very concerned about the book."

"Who?"

"Someone involved back then. Long before you or I ever thought we'd be in Key West."

"Do you know who it is?"

Padre Thomas shook his head and took another bite of his sandwich. "I warned Wizard yesterday. He told me he had an idea for protecting everyone and was supposed to pass it on to Tony this morning. He wouldn't tell me more, just not to worry."

"Tony should've worried," I sipped the warm *con leche*.

Padre Thomas put his sandwich down and lit a cigarette. "Wizard doesn't even know."

"How do you know?"

"He asked me if I had seen Tony."

"What did you say?"

"I told him no." He inhaled deeply. "Because I hadn't."

"Can you help the cops?" I finished the coffee.

"You know I can't," his grin returned. "At first they wouldn't believe anything I told them and then, since I'd give them information only the killer should know, they'd think I did it."

He had a point. In the past, his knowledge of things that happened in secret or dark places had gotten him in trouble. I was one of the few people he confided in, maybe because he knew I believed him about the angels, or at least wanted to.

My cell phone chirped. "Yeah."

"Mick, it's Tracy at the Hog's Breath," the words whispered hoarsely in my ear, like Lauren Bacall talked to Bogey in the movies. "One of those old treasure guys is here looking for you."

"Wizard?" It was too early for the Hog's bar to be open.

"No, the one they call Lucky."

"Where is he?"

"Downstairs." Tracy worked in the office on the second floor. "He left you something, but he's sitting at the bar waiting."

"Thanks, Tracy, I'll be there in a little while." I closed the cell phone.

"All three of those treasure hunters are in danger," Padre Thomas crushed out the cigarette and bit into the last of his sandwich. "Be careful, Mick."

"Tell me something I can use, Padre."

"They've scared someone from back then," he mumbled as he chewed. "Someone who'll kill to keep a secret."

"Thanks for the coffee," I got up and rode my bike down the harbor walk toward the Hog's Breath, having learned nothing from the Chief, but Padre Thomas explained it hadn't been Tony's past that caught up with him, it was someone else's.

~~~

It smelled and felt like rain, the humidity getting thick, as clouds blowing in from the south began to hide the morning sun. Key West had been getting afternoon showers everyday for almost a month and they brought a summer mugginess that reminded us we lived in the tropics as well as in the southernmost city in the Continental United States.

The Hog's Breath Saloon is a short block from the waterfront, at Duval and Front streets, but large hotels block any scenic view of the water. When cruise ships are in port their smokestacks rise above the hotels and are visible from the Hog's outdoor patio bar. It's a friendly place where the bartenders remember your name and what you drink after only a few visits and, because it's outdoors, smoking is allowed. I routinely meet friends there for cigars.

The parking lot between the bank and the Hog's Breath had two cars in it and the outdoor bar area looked empty. As I rode in off Duval Street, I thought Lucky got tired of waiting and left. I was wrong.

I locked my bike in the bike rack and headed in.

To the right of the parking lot entrance of the Hog there is a stage, to the left a small raw bar that also served draught beer. Straight ahead was the large full-service bar with seating on all four sides.

Lucky was sitting on the ground, bar stools were turned over, and a sword, thrust through his stomach, impaled him to the bar. A small pirate flag hung from its grip. Lucky's face showed pain and fear. Blood dripped in multiple spots down his T-shirt. I looked around, but there was no one. The *con leche* turned in my stomach. I walked to the side of the bar that faced the restaurant, so I wouldn't have to see Lucky, and called the Chief.

Next, I called Tracy upstairs.

"Tracy, there's going to be some police action downstairs," I took a deep breath, "stay upstairs, but call Charlie and tell him someone has died at the bar …"

"Mick!" She didn't let me finish. "Who?"

"You're going to have enough cops upstairs in a little while, just call Charlie and prepare yourself …"

"For what?" the gravelly whisper began to sound nervous. "What's happening?"

"Call Charlie, Tracy, and don't mention my package, please. All you know is Lucky asked for me, so you called me, nothing else. The cops are on their way. Put the package in the safe, please," I disconnected the call and lit a cigar. I needed the package and I trusted Tracy to put it away and keep our secret, but knew it would cost me a lunch and twenty questions, in a day or two.

A squad car screeched into the parking lot, lights flashing, and siren wailing. The Chief pulled in a few seconds behind and had the cop turn them off. He held the uniformed officer back and walked toward me. He stopped and looked down at Lucky, then motioned me to meet him.

"You said he was Lucky," he shook his head. "I guess he isn't anymore."

I chomped on the cigar, but there wasn't the foul odor that the boat cabin had, I was just nervous.

The Chief got closer and bent down to the body. "Stab wounds," he said, more to himself than to me.

"There's a trail of blood from the raw bar to where you are," I pointed to small splatters of blood on the cracked concrete floor.

"Why are you here?" he stood up. "Where you meeting him too?"

"I was having coffee with Padre Thomas and Tracy upstairs called and told me Lucky was here looking for me."

"The crazy priest! Don't you know any normal people?" he shook his head and watched the crime scene van drive in. "Did you touch anything? The sword?"

"You're the most normal person I know, Chief, and no, I didn't touch anything."

Sherlock stopped at the entrance and looked down at Lucky. He scanned the stage and the raw bar and he saw the blood spatters. He walked to where they began and waved the Chief over. Pretending he was holding a sword, Sherlock twirled his wrist and thrust forward like Errol Flynn in an old swashbuckling movie, forcing the Chief backward.

"Tell me something," he stabbed forward and the Chief backed up. "Tell me something, tell me something," he repeated as he thrust forward. In four or five steps the Chief had his back against the stage railing and Sherlock turned him to the bar, "Tell me something," he yelled and the Chief almost tripped over Lucky.

"The killer is getting messy and nervous," Sherlock said, dropping his imaginary sword. "There was a conversation, he didn't like what he heard, or didn't hear and killed the guy quickly and cleanly on the boat. Here, he stabbed the vic," he looked down at the body, "maybe six times from what I can see. He's after something or someone and he's getting nervous. Who's left of the three?"

"Wizard is back at the station, so we know he didn't do this," the Chief looked at me. "The other old guy is Bubba?"

"Yeah," I sat back down. "If he's not on his boat, he's probably at a bar."

The Chief took Sherlock's radio and called dispatch. He wanted Bubba picked up.

"What is it with the swords and pirate flags?" Sherlock checked behind the body.

"You know their story about finding the treasure, right?"

"Yeah, I've heard so many versions, I don't believe any of them."

"You're probably right," I took the cigar out of my mouth. "Tony was helping them write their memoirs and my guess is someone's afraid of something in the story."

"Why?" the Chief moved closer.

"If I knew that, I'd know who the killer is, wouldn't I?"

"This sword looks as old as the other one," Sherlock studied the sword handle. "There can't be that many pirate swords on the island ... maybe we're looking for a collector."

"Since the Pirate Soul museum opened there's no shortage of replicas," I said.

"Damn," he stood up. "Two bodies, two swords, it's gotta be the same killer," he pointed toward the sword and pirate flag, "who is scared and that makes him more dangerous than methodical. Unless you've got an idea about a suspect, Chief, I think you need to call FDLE."

"Yeah," he sat at a barstool, his back to the body. "But let's give our detectives a few hours on their own, maybe they'll come up with a suspect."

The Florida Department of Law Enforcement is like a state FBI and is used often by small municipalities in the Florida Keys when major crimes occur. Sherlock regularly uses the FDLE crime lab in his investigations.

"Someone at the marina must have seen something," I added in support.

"You're right there, Mick," Sherlock answered a little too quickly, "people saw you, but no one saw anyone before you got on the boat."

"Well, then," I stuffed the cigar back in my mouth, "they didn't see Tony get on, so they missed him, why not the killer?"

Two police cars pulled to a stop in the parking lot. It was time for the investigation to get going and I knew that meant talking to Tracy.

"Give your statement to the officer outside," the Chief said. "And come to the station when Luis calls you. Any idea why Lucky was looking for you here, when the bar's not open?"

"None," I lied.

"You were lookin' for the first vic and he got himself killed," Sherlock said flatly, "you were comin' to meet this vic, and he's dead. Do me a favor, Mick, go home and stop lookin' for people!"

~~~

I didn't go home, because I needed the package Lucky had left with Tracy. A section of the sky filled with rain clouds, but to the north, the sun shined. I rode my bike to Harpoon Harry's, knowing it would be hours before the police finished at the Hog's Breath.

The breakfast crowd had gone and it was too early for the lunch bunch, so I grabbed a table in back and Ron, the owner, brought me a mug of black coffee and the menu. I ordered an egg and cheese sandwich on Cuban bread.

"You mind if I join you?"

Attorney Shawn Eden stood there, a warm smile spread across his freshly shaven face. I was pouring sugar into my coffee and pointed at the empty seat across from me.

Shawn is a big man, in size and in the community. His thick mop of hair has turned gray, but once it was as black as his attorney's heart. His family has been in the Keys for forever and he is a Conch, the name given to local families that have lived here for generations. His dress code is colorful print shirts, creased linen pants, and expensive loafers without socks.

Ron brought him a mug of coffee and Shawn waved off the menu.

"A shame about your friend," he said and poured four spoons of sugar into his coffee. "I talked with him recently about my backing the treasure hunters." He couldn't stifle a laugh. "I don't mean to be disrespectful, but those guys were anything but treasure hunters."

"You made a lot of money off their treasure, counselor," I sipped my coffee.

"I met the three of them back in the '60s," he closed his eyes. "More than forty years ago. I was fresh out of law school and I had my degree. What you see here in Key West today, that's not what it was like when I can home." He pointed toward the harbor and Waterfront Market, "That area there was filled with shrimp boats, PT's was a tough country-western bar. And the shrimpers weren't bringing in much shrimp, but they had a lot of square groupers to unload," he laughed, again. "God, what a town this used to be."

Square groupers are bales of marijuana. Key West businessmen backed local fishermen and they made fortunes bringing in loads of marijuana from mother ships offshore. It went on into the 1980s, but then the smugglers switched to cocaine and the rules changed. The money was better, but DEA and Custom Agents where in Key West and family men were going away to do hard time in far off jails. It stopped being a sport everyone was involved in, about that time.

"You're right though, I made good money off their treasure," he sipped the coffee. "I never thought I would. I saw the three of them as colorful characters and tried to help them out with money. I thought of it as a handout, they considered it an investment in their businesses."

"Then you're lucky they looked at it that way."

"Well, yeah," he smiled. "For the derelict drunkards and liars they were, or are," he smiled again, "they turned out to be men of their words."

"They sign anything?" I began to nibble my sandwich.

"Never, we shook hands," he closed his eyes again. "I backed their bringing Conch in from the Bahamas and they scuttle their boat on some sandbar and ended up eating most of the Conch before the Coast Guard found them. I paid for them to get their captain's licenses so they could use one of their boats to take tourists to the reef. Hell, Mick, there had to be a dozen other schemes. I remember the day they walked into my office with some of their treasure and wanted me to be their partner."

"They needed money."

"You got that right. In all, I probably put in a little more than fifty grand," he grinned. "What a return on that investment."

"You know Lucky was murdered too," I watched him for a reaction. I didn't see one, but then he's an attorney and I am not sure they react to anything other than billing hours.

"Yeah, I got a call from the police."

Shawn's contacts went into all city departments and many local businesses, because he and his family owned a variety of businesses in Key West and the Upper Keys.

"Everyone knows I handle their legal affairs," he broke off a piece of my sandwich and ate it. "I do that pro bono, too."

"The cops have the Wizard and they're looking for Bubba."

"I know these guys, they couldn't kill anyone, they might drown you by mistake," he laughed, "but they couldn't kill anyone."

"Maybe it has something to do with the book?"

Shawn laughed clearly this time. "The book! Mick, it wouldn't be a memoir it would be a work of fiction. They haven't been in their right minds for forty years. Is that what the cops think?"

"I have no idea what the cops think."

"Yeah, but you found both bodies."

"I can't argue that, counselor, and I think I'm Sherlock's number one suspect."

"You're another one I'd lay money on couldn't kill someone."

"You know me, Shawn, I believe in running away so I can run another day."

"A man after my own heart. Hey, I need to get to the police station and see they aren't using a rubber hose on Wizard. I'll see you around," he stood up, said something to Ron and left.

I drank another cup of coffee, but still had a couple of hours before I could go back and get what Lucky had left with Tracy.

~~~

Light rain wet one side of Caroline Street, as I rode my bike toward Simonton Street, where I turned and then again on Fleming Street, going against the one-way traffic. The rain stayed at the waterfront. I locked my bike in front of Island Books.

Books, shelved and in stacks, filled the narrow store. Books about Key West, its history, and its characters ran along the right wall; and there were signed books by Key West authors on a display as you first came into the shop. New books, used books, picture books filled the store. In the next room, the condition was the same, books, and more books.

I saw Mitch's head through the open door to his small office in the back, he was working at his computer. There was no one at the register and two customers wondered through the store.

"You're here early," Mitch said. He must have had eyes in the back of his head.

"Have you heard about the two murders?"

He turned in his book-cramped office and stared at me. "In Key West?" Classical music played lightly from his computer speakers.

"Yeah, in Key West."

"Tell me," he pushed his glasses up on his noise and waited.

I told him and he listened quietly.

"Any suspects? I mean, besides you."

"Thanks," I said. "I don't know what they've done in the last few hours, maybe they do, maybe they don't."

"Are you hiding out?" he twisted in his chair.

"When they call me to come in for questioning I'll go in."

"Really? Take an attorney."

"I don't need one."

"Famous last words. Look it, if they've got no one else, then it has to be you. I beg your pardon, but that's how it works."

"I don't think so, Mitch. I have witnesses, there's no physical evidence ..."

"Coincidence, Mick," he pushed his glass back in place and stood up. "Take my advice and don't go to the police station without legal representation, coincidence has put others in jail."

Outside, I lit another cigar and decided to walk along Duval Street toward the Hog's Breath. I could see the rain clouds hovering at Lower Duval. Cars and scooters rushed in both directions and the sidewalks were busy with tourists. Outside Jimmy Buffett's Margaritaville Restaurant, people were lined up for lunch seating. At Fat Tuesday's early revelers enjoyed the toxic frozen drinks they served and across Caroline Street Fogerty's had its first lunch group seated. The island was busy for mid week. Rain was a block away.

The two hundred block of Duval was the party area, be it spring break or Fantasy Fest or any day of the week with a D in it. The Tree Bar, Angelina's Pizza, and Rick's were open and busy. Across the street, the Lazy Gecko, Sloppy Joe's Bar, and Irish Kevin's were just as busy. This block of Key West sold a good time by the glass and there was no shortage of takers. Rain drizzled across Greene Street, like a beaded curtain.

The bank's parking lot was full and the afternoon entertainment had begun at the Hog's Breath. Joel Nelson sat on the rain-protected stage and played for a half-full bar. We nodded at each other as I walked in. The bloodstains on the broken cement floor had been washed away and all the bar stools were upright. Kevin tended the raw bar and Irish Bob was alone behind the big bar.

"Interesting morning," Irish Bob said as I passed.

"How long have you been open?"

"About an hour," he smiled. "You gonna tell me about it?"

"Later, I need to go to the office," and I kept walking.

Tracy was alone.

"You owe me," she smiled, and put down what she was working on. "Hold on."

I closed the door as she walked into the back room. She came back holding a manila envelope.

"What's in it?" she handed it to me.

I opened the envelope and six audiotapes and a note from Tony slid out. I put them back.

"Thanks, Tracy. I'll let you know as soon as I listen to them. You okay?"

"Are you okay?" she sat down. "Morales had a lot of questions about you. I told him what I did, called you, and that was it. The son of a bitch doesn't believe me."

"His job is to be suspicious. Don't let him get to you."

"I had to sign my statement."

"Consider yourself lucky, I have to go to the station to give mine."

I stuffed the envelope against my back and walked out into the rain.

~~~

Tony's note echoed what Shawn had said about the book having better prospects of being a mystery novel rather than a memoir. The afternoon rain pounded the deck on my sailboat, the Fenian Bastard, as I pulled my small tape recorder from storage and played the tapes. I poured some Jameson over ice and sipped the drink as I listened.

The three treasure hunters had sat with Tony and told their stories; each cutting in on the other to make corrections, because they never seemed to agree. The most interesting parts were about smuggling marijuana and who had financed their frequent trips. They even named some of the Mexican boaters on the mother ship, as well as local backers, but again, they argued about that. Much of the information had been rumored for years around the island, so there was little new in the tapes.

It was almost humorous when they talked about discovering the treasure. They were diving, illegally, for local lobsters when they discovered the first few artifacts. It took them weeks of scrapping the bottom by hand to find more and then they took it to Shawn. They each respected Shawn for his years of support and always considered him their business partner.

I put a blank tape in my recorder, put my Glock, with a round in the chamber, in the pocket of my foul-weather jacket with the recorder, and called Chief Dowley. I told him where to meet me and left as the rain turned to drizzle. I had a good idea of who the killer was, but it didn't make any sense. Then again, murder rarely does.

~~~

Lightening flashed and thunder boomed, as I walked into the plush empty outer office. The inside door was open and classic music played from hidden speakers. I unzipped my jacket and turned the tape recorder on, as I walked through the open office door and closed it. Shawn sat at his clear glass-topped desk; a coke spoon in his hand came down empty from his nose. A small bag of white powder and a revolver sat on the desk.

"Do you want some?" His eyes stared hard at me, but he smiled.

"No Shawn, I have a hard enough time being a drunk."

"This is better than booze." He filled the small coke spoon and inhaled it through one nostril. "You have the tapes?"

"Yeah, I have them."

"The crazy bastards," he growled, "I didn't think they'd turn on me."

"They didn't."

He looked puzzled for a moment and then smiled again. "What do you mean?"

"You were right, Shawn," I moved away from the desk. "Mostly they argued on the tapes. Talked about their smuggling and joked about finding the treasure."

"They lied about me and my family, I know they did." He was becoming agitated.

"No they didn't, Shawn," I tried to say calmly. "There are more rumors out on the street about how Key West families got their money from square groupers, than are on the tapes."

"That's what Tony said. I didn't believe him, either."

"He told you that before you killed him?"

"Yeah," he growled again. "Now you're saying he told me the truth?"

"He wasn't going to write the memoir, he wanted to use the information for a mystery novel," I moved another step back.

"That's good news, but it's a little late." His laugh sounded like an animal's howl. "Of course, it's not good news for you, is it? You know the truth," he inhaled another spoonful of cocaine. "I have to kill you, and then this will go away."

"Are you going to run me through with a pirate sword, too?" I stood still and put my hand on the Glock.

"No, the swords are gone," he smiled. "Wizard had two of them and Tony made me so angry I just picked one up and drove it through him as he went to sit down."

"You took the other one with you to kill Lucky?" I wanted it all on tape.

"Tony told me Lucky was taking the tapes to you, so I went after him," he said quietly. "I didn't realize I had the other sword with me until I got to my car. I drove around and saw Lucky walk into the Hog and I parked around on Front Street," his hand was shaking so much he couldn't hold the coke spoon. "I waited for him by the parking lot and when he came down stairs, I confronted him and I still had the sword. He wouldn't go back for the tapes. Damn fool, he didn't think I'd do it, even after I stabbed him a few times."

"Shawn, it has to stop. You're connected enough to cop a manslaughter plea," I said for the tape recorder. "Turn yourself in."

He howled again and stood up, the revolver in his quivering hand. "It stops when you disappear, no sword, no body."

"It will be messy in here, Shawn, blood and noise."

"Let me worry about that," he said and stepped away from the desk. "Where are the tapes?"

"On my boat. You gonna go get them?" I watched his gun hand tremble.

"Unless you want to take me there," he laughed cruelly, his eyes wide.

I backed up, I wanted distance between us.

"You were wrong to worry about the book, Shawn, and wrong about me, too."

"Wrong about you, how?" He moved back toward a file cabinet, but held the gun aimed at me.

"I can kill, Shawn," I said calmly. "I can't run a sword through an innocent man, like you did, but I can kill to protect myself."

"Yeah? But I have the gun."

"Wrong again, Shawn," I kept calm and smiled. "I have a gun in my pocket and it's aimed at you."

"Show it to me," he challenged me angrily. "I don't believe you."

"Put the gun down, Shawn, and we'll both be alive when the police arrive."

"I still don't believe you," and he fired one shot that went past my left shoulder, his hand trembled. "Damn you!" He fired again and missed.

The two shots echoed and the room smelled of burnt cordite.

I fired the Glock and hit him square in the chest. The cocaine rush kept him standing, but he looked down at the growing bloodstain on his flowery shirt and then back at me. He raised his arm up, ready to fire again. I had the gun out of my pocket and pointed at him. I shook my head.

"No Shawn, drop it." He didn't and I shot him again, and my ears rang from the noise.

He fell against the file cabinet and slid to the floor. The door behind me crashed against the office wall as Chief Dowley rushed in, gun in hand. He looked at me and then at Shawn, who died with a cocaine smile.

"Damn, Mick, I hope you're right," he said softly. "You just killed an important guy."

I pulled the tape recorder out of my pocket and handed it to him. I heard sirens from outside. "Yeah, in self defense and I solved two murders for you."

He took my Glock, put it on a chair, and then rewound the tape. Two uniformed officers came in, guns drawn.

"Call the paramedics," he told them and led me into the outer office. "He confesses on this?"

"And fired first, it's all there."

He placed the recorder next to his ear and played the tape. He smiled. "Why didn't you wait for me?"

"I hoped I was wrong."

"So why call me to meet you here?"

"If I was wrong I was gonna buy you beer."

He put the recorder in his pocket and talked to the uniformed officer at the door. Chief Dowley waved me over and led me outside.

"Let me buy you a drink, after all, this is Key West, not Miami and you ain't goin' anywhere. Hell, Mick, it's been one long day," he put his arm around my shoulder, "and I can use a beer. Then we have to go see Luis for your statement."

"They guy hates me, Chief," I allowed him to tug me toward the street.

"Yeah, but I still love you."

"What about my gun?"

"It's in an evidence bag," he said and we walked away in the rain.

2. A Lucky Man

Jonathan Woods

For me the coins have always landed heads up. An inherited fortune doubled by my own efforts before I turned 50, a beautiful wife, two intelligent children, and a plethora of skanky executive assistants, male and female, ready to fetch me cappuccinos or single malts, sharpen my pencils or hop into bed on a moment's notice.

All so regular and predictable.

Brian Midnight is the name I sign on letters and legal documents. I'm in the private equity business. Midnight Enterprises, Inc. is the name of my company. Behind my back at the racquet club and other hotbeds of snobbery around town, I've been called a bloodsucking raider and worse. Fuck 'em!

What I craved was true excitement. A plague from the Orient. A giant meteor hurtling toward the earth. Something to get my blood pulsing, my cock stiff as an Irish shillelagh.

That Friday, as was my usual habit, I strode into the office at five minutes to nine. Through its floor to ceiling glass panels I beheld a sterling vista up and down the polluted Hudson and, on the farther shore, of the wastelands of the Jersey salt marshes, Newark's urban blight and beyond, to the boring heartland, the yellow haze of L.A. and, on the far horizon, Japan, with its teeming millions churning out flat screen TVs and Ramen noodles.

It was a breezy October day with heavy rain-laden clouds scudding like sharks across the sea-gray sky.

By eleven I completed lengthy conference calls with my London and Zurich offices and signed a dozen contracts and letters laid before me by my extraordinarily buxom executive assistant of the moment. Her name was Muriel.

At last I deep-sixed the Zurich call and, swinging around in my antique executive chair, rested the heels of my spit-polished Berluti toe-capped black oxfords on the edge of my desk. Massive and fashioned of the most endangered Malaysian teak, the kidney-shaped desk might have been ripped from the bowels of some giant primordial ape, from King Kong himself.

With a melancholy puff of breath, I gazed upward hoping perhaps for some visitation, like Scrooge and his ghosts. Instead my eyes locked on the lewd, bulbous body of a bluebottle fly circling in the slipstream of the air conditioning, moving lazily around and through the gently twisting leaves of a Calder mobile hung from the ceiling. How the hell had this grotesquery gotten into my office? If I'd had a .45 handy, I'd have blown the fucker to kingdom come.

As I contemplated the fly's demise, Muriel entered my personal space bearing a hand-carved, ivory-inlaid humidor. From its aromatic interior I selected a fat, smooth-wrapped Cohiba not unlike the cured prick of some Cuban gigolo whose rakish days had been cut short by a jealous husband. Deftly she trimmed the end and, leaning forward to give me an ample glimpse of her attributes, set the cigar between my churlish lips. The executive assistant in training, a sandy-haired lad bearing a striking resemblance to the young Steve McQueen of old, stepped from behind Muriel and fired up a gold Dunhill lighter. Since the position of executive assistant in training was virtually *pro bono*, Russell taught zumba classes and engaged in other less savory undertakings on the side to pay the rent. The tip of the Cohiba sizzled and glowed a brilliant orange, as I drew in the calming smoke.

"Get a can of bug spray and exterminate that fucking fly," I said.

Then my phone rang.

Muriel answered; listened for a moment with one eyebrow arched archly. "I'll see if he's available," she said. As her hand covered the speaker, a sudden streak of sunlight broke through the drear October sky and exploded in ice-blue sparks on her cerulean lacquered nails. I reached for my Ray-Bans.

"It's Chad," she said.

Chad is my son. My wife Grace picked the name. She thought it sounded aristocratic. For me it conjured up derelict images of a landlocked African shit hole. Our daughter's named Jacqueline (after you know whom) and is in her second year at Yale Law. Chad's a freshman at Pepperdine.

I took the phone.

"Chad, my boy. You're up with the Waste Management crews. Are you doing a ride along? Or just getting in from an all night prowl?"

Chad was the spitting image of his old man. Liked to take a walk on the wild side.

"Actually, dad, I'm in the Dean's Office. I'm being expelled."

"Good god. Not for some left wing devilment, I hope."

"My roommate and I were trying to cook up a batch of meth as a science experiment. Just to see if we could do it."

"A bad choice. Better you should be growing pot in California. It's virtually legal out there."

"They're not turning me over to the cops or pressing charges. They just want me on the next plane back East."

"Well then, no harm, no foul. Besides, it's perfect timing. I was just heading down to the Keys for a little sport fishing. You can join me. I'll have Muriel book you a flight from L.A. to Key West.

"Swell, dad. I knew you'd understand. Who's Muriel?"

"My new executive assistant. She keeps me on the straight and narrow."

The call ended. Well, at least he hadn't blown up the fucking dorm, I thought, as I sucked in another mellow mouthful of cigar smoke.

Muriel was standing by. I caught her attention. "Call the airstrip and tell them to gas up the Jetstream. Book Chad first class from LAX to the Conch Republic. Then call Captain Bob and tell him to sober up cause we're comin' down to do some badass bonefishing." With a leer I grabbed and shook the crotch of my hand-tailored sharkskin suit.

~~~

Grace was pissed when I phoned and told her I had to go south for an emergency business negotiation. One of the many charities whose affairs kept her busy was having a fancy dress reception at the MoMA that very evening and I wouldn't be there decked out in a monkey suit to toast the chairperson with my usual blithe and witty words.

"But Brian, you've known about tonight's festivities for weeks," she whined.

"Business is business," I said. "There's nothing I can do. I'll call Gabe. I'm sure he'll be willing to fill in. You like Gabe."

Gabriel Smith was a blueblood lawyer and a drinking buddy of mine for more than twenty years. Over that time I'd thrown a lot of business his way. I'm one of the reasons he has a corner office at his Wall Street firm. Gabe's a very charming confirmed bachelor. He knows how to play Grace like a piano concerto, sending shivers up and down her spine.

"When will you be back?" There was a thud of resignation in Grace's voice.

"Hard to say."

"Well, don't call me tonight. I'll be out late and I'm sure I'll have too much to drink."

And no doubt get your furrow plowed by a member of the bar, I thought.

"I'm sorry, darling," I said. "I'm sure the evening will be a great success even without me."

But the line was already dead.

On the ride out to the private airport on Long Island where I kept the Jetstream, I read the Wall Street Journal and the Financial Times and drank two Tanqueray martinis. Russell was an excellent driver but not much in the chitchat department. I always kept a weekender stocked with Orvis sportswear stashed on the corporate jet for unplanned getaway opportunities.

I slept on the flight down and by eight p.m. I was at the outside bar at Louie's Backyard in quaint Key West, waiting for Chad to arrive. A mosquito, no doubt bearing deadly dengue fever spoors, buzzed by my ear. With a swipe I caught him in the palm of one hand, crushing him into a blood red dot of oblivion.

Chad arrived at nine-thirty on the last puddle hopper from Miami and fifteen minutes later sat on the stool next to mine sucking down a cool Heineken. We closed down the bar at Louie's and wandered up Whitehead Street to do some serious drinking at the Green Parrot. Chad wanted to celebrate his good fortune not to be languishing in a Malibu jail cell. I've always been up for a night of boozing on a moments notice. We rolled back into the Casa about three a.m.

~~~

It was a little after ten Saturday morning when Captain Bob finally cranked up the Evinrude and headed his shallow-draft skiff out of the slip on Stock Island and turned up the Keys toward bonefish country. In a hungover haze, Chad slumped amidships, sipping on his second *colada* of the morning. That's Cuban for four shots of espresso strong enough to wake a zombie.

As Captain Bob's callused and age-spotted hand bore down on the throttle, I sat in the skiff's bow feeling the nautical breeze ruffle my carefully-tended locks, daydreaming about the flame-eyed bubba chick who'd been scanning me from a bar stool at the Parrot the night before. Bonding with my offspring had held me back from testing the depths of her interest, but she was a great mental fuck.

Captain Bob himself was fairly the worse for wear. Hunkered down by the aft guide platform, his hulking, hairy form draped in weathered khakis reminded me of an obese orangutan dressed up for a tea party. His bloated, sagging visage could easily have been from a corpse three days in the water. One wandering eye squinted into the sun, the other so red and swollen shut from some recent brawl, it looked like the last wizened apple at the bottom of the barrel after a long, hard winter. An ancient ship's officer cap was drawn rakishly over his drab, grey-streaked curls that looked like they'd been trimmed by a psychopath armed with a dull straight razor.

So much for being bright eyed and bushy tailed as we set forth to partake of the greatest sport fishing in the world, fly casting for the elusive and paranoid bonefish.

Somewhere near lower Sugarloaf Key, Captain Bob veered through a narrow mangrove-edged channel that brought us out on the Gulf side. Ahead the palest turquoise water shimmered and slid in a broad cascading array over white sand flats. Captain Bob killed the Evinrude and tilted it out of the water before it hit bottom. With a groan he mounted the guide platform and began to pole us over the knee-deep waters of the flats, his one good eye panning across 180 degrees for the telltale flicker of a bonefish tailfin.

Rod in hand, line baited with a redbone fluff fly, I waited on Captain Bob's whispered alert that a wily bonefish was in the offing.

Three hours later, with nary a sighting, my enthusiasm was beginning to materially sag. The imperious tropical sun beat down relentlessly like the cat-o-nine-tails of the Marquis de Sade.

Chad, having early on lost interest in the possibilities of bonefishing, had taken off his shirt, chugged two beers from the cooler and fallen asleep in the blazing sun in his minimal swim trunks. His only signs of life were the occasional flop from back to stomach or the reverse, to ensure that he was evenly burned on every surface. Yours truly, not being a total greenhorn, had dressed for success in a wintergreen-colored Orvis ultraviolet-ray-resistant, long-sleeved fisherman's shirt, jeans and a wide brimmed straw Panama. I kept slathering on quantities of creamy, ill-smelling sunscreen sufficient to turn me into a giant walking coconut in a pina colada TV ad.

Captain Bob just kept poling and scanning, his leathery, reptilian skin deflecting all ill effects of the sun's rays. Not a discouraging word or any other escaped his sunbaked lips. I began to wonder whether he had drifted into some catatonic limbo state, halfway between being and nothingness.

The monotony of the business was starting to weigh on my soul. I could feel rage rising in my gut at the chimerical bonefish I knew were taunting us from the shimmering horizon. They were out there, laughing at us, if fish could laugh. If a school of the "grey ghosts of the flats," as Zane Grey once described them, had flitted by at that moment, I would have happily dropped a grenade in their midst.

Relax, I cautioned myself. You're on vacation. You love sport fishing.

Reaching into the breast pocket of my shirt, I extracted a medium sized spliff and fired it up. It seemed like seconds later (or was it hours?) that I heard a gravelly whisper:

"Eleven o'clock, about 70 feet out. Near the patch of floating seaweed."

Was I hallucinating? No! It was Captain Bob. We had a live one!

Cautiously, I rose to a standing position. Didn't want to scare the little bastard with any sudden movements.

Now I saw him. The quicksilver flash of a tailfin partially out of water just to the left of a clump of gulfweed. I draw my rod back over my shoulder, my wrist whipping backward to make the cast, sending the weighted line first circling behind, then hurtling forward toward the flickering shadow of the target.

Next moment a deep, gurgling howl of pain and rage rose up behind me. My head snapped around, my eyes blinking in disbelief. The barbed hook of my fluff fly had snagged Captain Bob's good eye and the force of my forward cast had yanked the eyeball from its socket!

Captain Bob's arms flew up in a flurry of flailing activity, vainly seeking to retrieve the missing eyeball. Blind, or nearly so, he tottered left, then right, his mouth agape and slobbering like some primordial fish out of water. One deck-shoe-shod foot slipped off the edge of the guide platform and Captain Bob pitched sideways in slow motion, landing in an explosion of seawater.

Chad lurched to his feet.

"What the fuck!"

"His eye, it's his eye!" I screamed, jumping up and down and madly reeling in the line from my fatal cast.

"What the fuck are you talking about, dad? Whose eye?"

"Captain Bob's," I said.

I had fully rewound my line. The rusty-red fluff fly was still attached to the end, but the eye was gone. It was out there somewhere, maybe floating like a cork. Did eyeballs float? Or rolling lazily across the sandy bottom. Or had the bonefish gobbled it up in a macabre feeding frenzy?

Then we looked at Captain Bob.

His khaki-covered bulk slumped face down in the shallow water like a bag of trash tossed from a passing luxury yacht. Captain Bob was a goner.

~~~

By the time we got done with the Coast Guard and the Police and caught a taxi back to the Casa Marina Resort, it was after six p.m. The dying sun cast the sky in lurid ribbons of blood.

"I feel like shit," said Chad, as the doorman swung wide the door to the Casa's grand lobby. "I think I soaked up a tad too much sun."

Indeed, Chad looked like he'd been slow-barbecued on an open spit for hours, which was pretty close to the truth. Once we were in our suite, he lay on the bed moaning, a wet washcloth laid across his forehead. After slathering Chad's pulsing Day-Glo pink flesh with aloe gel, I took a shower and put on shorts and a silk sport shirt decorated with images of retro yachts and pin-up girls.

Chad had fallen into a fever doze. I was on my own for the evening, which suited me just fine. Who knew what mischief I might get up to of the old lingam and yoni variety?

~~~

The evening was as lush and humid as a Turkish steam bath in a 1940s gay spy movie. I took an open-air pedicab to the raucous end of Duval Street. On the front porch of a Victorian mansion that was now a pretentious eatery, I drank my usual deuce of Tanqueray martinis and chomped my way through a house salad with chunky blue cheese dressing and a ten-ounce New York strip, seared on the outside, bloody in. I ignored the medley of seasonal vegetables and the tepid fries and flirted shamelessly with the blowsy blonde with the great ass assigned to cater to my wants. From the height of the old mansion's porch, I had a perfect view of the comings and goings of the mélange of tourists and party animals, hustlers and dealers, pimps and poontang that crowded the sidewalks and spilled into the street, looking for five minutes of happiness or a quick speedball fix.

When my waitress, sipping a brandy, sat down at my table and told me she got off in fifteen minutes, I took a pass and joined the milling throng. Suddenly tangled up in the rotting intestines of futility and ennui, I wandered aimlessly amid the revelers.

Poor Captain Bob. A pathetic finish to a legendary career as a fishing guide. On the other hand was there any way to kick the bucket that wasn't humiliating and degrading? What glory was there in being blown to smithereens on the battlefield, gasping your last breath with your guts spilling out like a mess of chitlins waiting to be boiled up and seasoned with hot sauce? You died with the same gurgling death rattle, whether lying alone and forgotten in a shotgun shack on the wrong side of town or in the palatial half-acre bedroom of your vast estate surrounded by groveling, greed-hungry relatives and retainers.

God damn it! I wasn't ready for that quite yet.

A blues band was making a ruckus at the Green Parrot, but I wasn't in the mood. The bubba chick who had taken my fancy the night before was nowhere to be seen. I turned away, walking instead down a quiet byway. As luck would have it, up ahead out of the darkness, a blue neon sign appeared in the window of a clapboard shack. It read: PSYCHIC READER & ADVISOR.

A chill tiptoed up my spine like black cat feet. I brushed it aside. Grace was big on signs and portents, horoscopes and fortune cookies, zodiacal conditions and the phases of the moon, diet pills and Botox. Me? I believed in balance sheets, patent rights and hard-edged business decisions. But in my present desultory mood, having my fortune read might be just what I needed to clear the air. It would be a hoot to joust with some charlatan over the casting of the runes.

I entered.

A single lamp draped in a shroud cast a thin light. In the shadowy interior I became aware of a man seated at a small, round table. His hands were folded together on the tabletop in front of him. His face was dark and pockmarked like toad skin. Above toad lips a waxed mustache from another era twirled in eccentric twists and curlicues. Longish pitch-black hair, slicked back like the demonic count in some cheesy gothic horror movie, glistened like lacquer in the gypsy light. Eyes like pitted black olives, on either side of nostrils infested with wiry caterpillar hairs, stared into nothingness. Was he asleep or in some drugged nirvana? I didn't give a shit one way or the other. In fact, why the fuck was I here? I turned to leave.

"Please have a seat." He spoke English in that high-pitched and abbreviated style of a pilgrim from the subcontinent. I've never been gung-ho about East Indians. They always seemed shady to me. Midnight Enterprises had once gotten entangled in a joint venture with a Mumbai-based company. It was a fucking disaster. We cut our losses and bailed.

His smile glinted like a knife blade. He motioned to the empty seat at the table. "Please."

"OK. Why not," I muttered. I sat down.

"Twenty dollars," the Indian said.

"I think I have a coupon." I started ruffling through my pockets.

"No coupon!" he said. He was ready to pick a fight. Next moment he leaned sideways and lit a stick of incense. The scent was as intense as sniffing pussy. "But I will give you an extra ten minutes free." He winked.

"OK. No coupon." I dropped a twenty on the table. It disappeared.

Suddenly the swami reached out and grabbed my hand, pulling it toward him.

I resisted. He pulled harder.

"I read your palm," he said, as if that made everything okay. "Tell your future. Love life. Money."

"Swell," I said. "Go for it."

"Maybe you want a drink?" the fortune-teller asked.

With one hand he set two shot glasses on the exotic hand-embroidered tablecloth. The cloth was covered in scarifying, otherworldly beings and arcane symbols, like something out of an H.P. Lovecraft horror story. A bottle appeared. He removed the cork with his teeth and poured. He was still holding my hand, as if in a vise.

"So," he said. "What is it you want to know?"

I drank my drink. The palm-reader jerked my hand into the faint aura cast by the lamp and stared hard at the palm.

"Have at it," I said.

"OK, this is what I see," he said. "You are a successful businessman. You travel. You have one, no, two kids. Your wife doesn't like sex much any more. And you are a twat hound."

Christ, I thought. This guy was pathetic. I'd paid twenty bucks for this bullshit?

"Anyone could lay that line of horse manure on me. I want to know about tonight," I said, "Tell me what's going to happen tonight."

"Hold still." He pulled my hand closer to the lamp, tracing the lines with his eyes. Then he looked intently into my face. I met his stare.

"I see a beautiful woman. She will drive you out of your mind."

"Come on, pal. You can do better than that."

"She will fuck your brains out."

"I can go with that."

"I see danger."

Danger! Danger was what I lived for. And the night was still young.

"You..." The seer's voice trailed off.

Then something weird happened. As I laughed and let my testosterone-jacked gaze intersect with the charlatan's walleyed orbs, a metal door slammed shut behind his eyeballs. Fear bled across his face like brake fluid at a fatal accident. Then nothing.

"What is it?" I asked.

He let go of my hand. I could still feel his grip imbedded in my hand's memory.

"All done," the fortune-teller said abruptly. "Very nice. Good night."

He stood and ducked through an opening in the black drapes covering the room's back wall. I was alone. Just me and the round table and the lamp and, on a shelf I hadn't previously noticed, a glass jar in which a two-headed fetus floated in an embryonic sea of formaldehyde.

What the fuck? I'd been cheated!

Then, unaccountably, a sense of dread washed over me.

With haste I left the shop and ran down the narrow lane until I was again amid the ebb and flow of the crowds on Duval

Street. I felt creeped out. Maybe like Chad, I'd gotten too much sun. Or was I still in shock from Captain Bob's swan dive?

I should check on Chad, I thought. Call it an early night.

Then again, there was the swami's vision of me and some Key West hottie screwing to beat the band.

Partway back to the Casa Marina, I passed an Italian restaurant. The idea of sipping a Sambuca became an *idée fixe*. A short video passed through my head: two priests in their black uniforms, and wearing wide straw hats, strolling down a nudist beach somewhere in southern Italy. Where had that come from?

When I walked into the otherwise empty bar, she was leaning over it, French kissing the barmaid, her flame-red hair like a biblical vision. She broke free and looked over at me. I thought at first she had been struck by lightning. A jagged white scar ran beneath her nose like a vein of quartz, splitting her face in two. Comedy on one side, Tragedy on the other. Then it occurred to me she had been born with a cleft palate and some butcher had had his way with her. Her tobacco-spit colored eyes laughed at me. She didn't care one way or the other whether she fucked my brains out or the opposite. Taking into account the barmaid, maybe a ménage à trois was in the cards, though the swami hadn't mentioned it.

Then she smiled her crooked smile at me. It was so real, so genuine, I lost my equilibrium and stumbled toward the zinc bar, crashing into a pair of stools.

"Hey," she said. "You doin' alright?"

I bought her a Jack neat and a Sambuca for myself; we watched the three espresso coffee beans float in the clear liquor, three tanned skinny-dippers.

Kelly was her name. An Irish father, a Cuban mother. When she talked she put her hand on my arm or hand or leg. Soon enough she had her hand on my cock, then she had the zipper down and my dick waltzed out in public. Next thing, I came all over her hand.

"Jeez Louise, don't get so excited."

"What did you expect when you took it out?" I asked.

The barmaid, whose name was Zoe, leaned across the bar and handed Kelly a wet towel. She eyed my declining johnson. I tucked him away. "If I was you," she said, "I'd get a motel room."

~~~

When Kelly and I walked into the lobby of the Casa, the assistant night manager rushed up, eyes leaping out of his head.

"Mr. Midnight, Mr. Midnight, Mr. Midnight."

"Spit it out, Ishmael," I said, slapping him on the back.

"Chad, sir. Your son, Chad."

"Yes. Chad. What about him?" Kelly's hand was rummaging in my front pocket like a hamster on its exercise wheel.

"I think he'll be fine, Mr. Midnight."

"Fine? What the fuck are you talking about!?"

Ishmael's eyes had zeroed in on my crotch and all the activity there. I jerked Kelly's predacious hand free of my trousers and twisted it until she bent halfway to the floor, cursing me.

I let her go and, turning back to Ishmael, slapped him twice across the face, back and forth. Whap, whap, like waves against the side of a boat.

"Tell me what the fuck is going on with Chad before I break your nose."

"He's in the hospital. Heatstroke. He was wandering around the lobby in sheer nylon skivvies. Asking attractive female guests weird questions, like what country was he in. We called 9-1-1. They took him to emergency over at the Medical Center."

My nerves were in overload. Sweat swept over my body; suddenly turned to ice. Chad, my sole male offspring, stricken. Could you die from heatstroke? Suffer irreversible brain damage?

Ishmael and the night manager calmed me down. I sat in the manager's comfy leather chair, behind the manager's desk in the manager's office smoking a Montecristo blunt from the manager's private stash, while they got the doctor on the phone. His name was Vishnu. Ishmael handed me the phone.

"Hello, this is Dr. Vishnu."

"Brian Midnight speaking. I'm Chad's father. I want to know how he is. No bullshit. Tell it to me straight up." I took a sip of the Patron tequila anejo that Ishmael had brought from the bar. In a pout Kelly slumped in the far corner of the lobby.

"Seriously dehydrated, sunburned over 80% of his body, running a temperature of 103. We have him on IV and ice packs. Should be ready to rock and roll in a day or two."

"And his brain?" I asked.

"As far as I know it's still there."

"What kind of joker are you?" I snarled.

"Relax, Mr. Midnight, you're in the tropics. This is laid-back Key West. No worries, maaahn. Your son's going to be fine. Enjoy the rest of your evening. Go look for your lost shaker of salt."

Chad was going to be fine! Tears of relief drizzled my cheeks. Enjoy the rest of your evening.

Fuck, yeah!

I grabbed a handful of Montecristos as I left the manager's office, stuffing them in the pockets of my shorts. That should confuse Kelly, I thought, as I walked toward her.

She ignored me, pretending to be reading that day's Key West Citizen. I ripped the newspaper out of her hands and tore it to shreds. Kelly leaped up and tried to slap me. I twisted her around and, with both her hands in my iron grip yanked back over her head, I quick-marched her to the elevator. When we emerged on the second floor, we were both smoking Montecristos and she was laughing at a dirty joke I'd just told about a Rabbi, a hooker and a penguin.

I ordered caviar and champagne from room service. Told them to hustle. Then I got naked and sat on the couch watching Seinfeld while Kelly took a shower. I had a hard-on that wouldn't quit. The sound of the pelting water in the shower reminded me of that old movie starring Marilyn Monroe and Joseph Cotton. What was it called? *Niagara*.

The caviar and champagne arrived. I spread super-salty, black fish eggs on a flaccid toast point daubed with sour cream. Added crumbled hardboiled egg. The toast triangle fit perfectly in my wide mouth. My taste buds sizzled. Heaven.

The shower stopped. Kelly's scarred face looked at me from around the edge of the bathroom door. Steam billowed forth. She saw my erection and cast me her winsome smile. When she walked into the room, a nine-inch, satanic-red dildo strapped to her loins, I knew what it felt like to be a sex object.

~~~

After a night of Sybaritic shenanigans, I left a snoring Kelly splayed amid sweat-soaked bed sheets, ordered a full breakfast for two from room service, and turned on the shower. Half an hour later, as I toweled off, the doorbell rang. Slipping into a fresh T-shirt and the previous evening's shorts, I threw open the door to the corridor. I found myself gazing not at the obsequious eyes of a hotel minion bearing breakfast, but into the cold, evil Cyclopean eye of an enormous black handgun pointing at the middle of my forehead. Shit!

Behind the gun I espied none other than my beautiful, if slightly going to seed, and now completely psycho, spouse. Her plump lips were twisted in a wolfish snarl. Using the weapon as a prod, she motioned me backwards, entering the room and closing the door behind her.

"You swine!" she spat.

"What are you doing here, Grace?" I asked.

"I came to put you out of your oversexed misery."

I decided to stick to my original cover story until I could come up with something better. "I'm down here on business," I said. "Strictly business."

There was a little moan from the bedroom, as of someone pleasuring themselves. Then Kelly's lyrical voice called out: "Brian, darling, is breakfast here?"

"That's not Chad," said Grace. "Who the fuck is that!? Some pussy you picked up at the negotiating table?" Her eyes grew huge and round. In their depths rage caught fire with the fury of an accelerant triggered by an arsonist's match.

"Chad's in the hospital," I said, hoping that information would divert Grace from her murderous thoughts.

Grace jerked spastically.

"Hospital? What are you talking about? Russell, your fucking assistant in training, told me you and Chad were down here on a sport fishing boondoggle. And I know what that entails. Drinking and whoring."

"How do you know Russell?" I asked in disbelief.

"He was the substitute instructor for my Saturday morning zumba class."

"Jesus."

"Now tell me why Chad's in the hospital before I shoot your pecker off."

"He got too much sun yesterday when we were out fishing on the flats."

"Too much sun? You are such a worthless piece of shit. You can't even look out for the well being of your own son."

At that moment Kelly appeared in the bedroom doorway. Naturally she was stark naked, her red hair disheveled, her equally bright red bush an utter distraction.

"I knew it!" yelled Grace, waving the handgun wildly back and forth between the two of us. "This is your last peccadillo at my expense. I'm taking you for every cent you own."

I raised one hand in a conciliatory motion.

"Grace. Let's be rational about this. If you go for a divorce, it will be all over Gawker and the New York Post. You'll be an outcast from all your society friends. This was just a boys-will-be-boys weekend getaway. Just pretend it never happened. I'll make it up to you. We'll go to Paris for a week, stay at the George V...."

Blam!

The gunshot was deafening in the enclosed space. A ragged hole appeared in the wall above the bedroom door. For a moment Kelly froze, a wax dummy in a Ripley's Believe It Or Not diorama. Next instant she broke into a wild-assed sprint, legs and arms flailing, eyes crazed by terror, white teeth clenched in a death's head grimace, aimed on a collision course with Grace, whose diminutive figure blocked the suite's exit. Lowering one shoulder, Kelly barreled full steam into Grace, knocking her on her ass, and just kept going, her gorgeous legs and buttocks pumping from side to side like the pistons of some slightly obscene Italian racecar. She ripped open the suite door and was gone with the wind.

Grace was in a sitting position, her dress twisted up around her waist, blood dripping down her chin from a split lip or some other injury. One hand still held the deadly weapon. Her eyes looked at me, murder rampaging in their depths.

The fucking fortuneteller from the night before hadn't mentioned anything about Grace arriving out of the blue, bent on mayhem. But one thing was clear: now was not the time for idle chitchat.

I turned tail and ran.

From the bedroom I burst through French doors onto the balcony. At the balcony's edge a drainpipe at one corner descended to the ground. A glance over my shoulder revealed Grace coming through the French doors like a berserk baboon. I only had one option. Vaulting the balcony railing, I swung onto the drainpipe and shimmied downward hand over hand until my feet touched solid ground.

Insane as it may sound, Grace roiled over the balcony edge and began to clamber down the drainpipe after me, like something out of Mission: Impossible.

I turned and sprinted through the Casa lobby, out the front doors and down the drive, heading for Higgs Beach. Unrelenting, Grace came after me, her running shoes eating up the pavement. Barefoot, I was at a serious disadvantage, stumbling over fallen palm fronds and other debris, razor glass and sharp-edged stones cutting and bruising my flesh.

Even as I heard the loud report of another shot fired, I swear I felt a rush of air as the bullet whizzed past my head.

This was no good.

With a surge of adrenalin I turned, a cornered beast, glancing hither and yon for some means of salvation. Grace was coming on like a demon from Hell, a mere dozen steps behind me. At my feet lay a brown, hard-shelled coconut like a shrunken head. Without thought I scooped up the coconut and hurled it with all my strength at the charging, blood-hungry beast that Grace had become. The coconut and Grace's skull connected with a sharp cracking sound. Her body withered to the pavement like a popped balloon.

I gaped. Then knelt by her fallen figure. A line of blood ran across her right temple where the impact of the coconut had torn the skin. Her eyes had rolled back. It didn't look good. I felt for the pulse of her carotid artery. Nada. Grace had gone to the happy hunting ground.

Now what the fuck was I going to do?

I saw the sleek blue steel killing machine lying in the white sand. Scooping it up and setting it firmly in the waistband of my shorts where my overlapping T-shirt concealed it from view, I walked rapidly into the nearby neighborhood.

~~~

I spent the day in several of Key West's lowlife bars, drinking heavily, bemoaning the fetid nightmare my life had morphed into. As the day waned, I grew more angry and despairing with each emptied shot glass. Was there a warrant out for my arrest for the murder of Grace Midnight? Or by some miracle had her death been ruled accidental. I imagined the headline in the next day's edition of the Key West Citizen: "Tourist struck dead by falling coconut."

As darkness trickled like thick molasses over the narrow streets and byways of old Key West, rage consumed me. Not at poor dead Grace. Nor at my own pussy-driven existence. Nor at the rotten hand the fates had dealt me.

No. My rage fell on one person and one person only. The fucking palm reader. I knew that last night, when he had abruptly ended our session, he had seen the future. He had seen Grace, armed to the teeth, arriving at the Casa, barging her way into my room, bringing ruin on my life. Driven by his own black heart, the soothsayer had chosen not to warn me, leaving me to stumble blindly into the unknown future where I had no choice but to murder my wife.

Suddenly I was no longer drunk. My senses were diamond sharp. It was time for payback.

With the utmost clarity I sought out the alleyway where the swami plied his nefarious trade. Ahead I saw the blue neon sign: PSYCHIC READER & ADVISOR.

I entered.

As before, the palm reader sat at the small round table. This time his hands were out of sight. His eyes flickered in the lamplight, as if consumed by fever.

"You forgot to tell me something last night, asshole," I said. "You forgot to mention that my wife would arrive unexpectedly." I paused for effect. "And end up dead by my own hand."

The swami's gaze never left mine. "That is true, mister." He spoke in a quivering voice. "And the other part I did not mention to you is, when you came to kill me, I shot you first."

Before I could react, he pulled the trigger of a small caliber pistol he held beneath the table.

But in his high-strung state, his aim faltered and the bullet only grazed my left thigh.

He looked surprised that I didn't fall over dead.

"I guess you should have turned one more page, pal," I said, putting two bullets through his heart.

As I walked back down the alley toward the noise and clamor of Duval Street, a great heaviness lifted from my body like an exhaled breath. With a handpicked team of defense lawyers and a brown bag or two of cash slipped to select jurors, I figured I had an excellent chance of beating both raps.

I was willing to admit that Grace had scored a point. That I wasn't the most attentive parent.

But I could work on that.

Suddenly I felt lucky again.

3. The Itinerary

Roberta Isleib
Writing as Lucy Burdette

Detective Jack Meigs knew he'd hate Key West the moment he was greeted off the plane by a taxi driver with a parrot on his shoulder. He hadn't wanted to take a vacation at all, and he certainly hadn't wanted to come to Florida, which he associated with elderly people pretending they weren't declining. But his boss insisted, and then his sister surprised him with a nonrefundable ticket: He was screwed. A psychologist had once told him that it took a year for grief to lift, and that making major life changes during this time only complicated the process. Which was why he'd gone to work directly from the funeral, and every day in the three months since. There was no vacation from the facts: His wife Alice was dead and she wasn't coming back.

The driver packed him into a cab that smelled like a zoo and lurched away from the curb. Then the bird let loose a stream of shit that splattered off his newspapered roost and onto Meigs's polished black leather loafers. The cabbie hooted with laughter.

"That means good luck, man," he said, gunning the motor and grinning like a monkey in the rear view mirror. "Mango doesn't do that for just anybody."

The parrot screamed during the entire ten-minute ride to Meigs's hotel and the driver never shut up either. Would everyone connected with this damn town want to give him a travelogue?

"I'm takin' you down our main street, give you the flavor," the cabbie said as he turned off Truman Avenue onto bustling Duval Street. He veered around a stumbling bum and a covey of fat, sun-crisped cruise ship escapees carrying plastic cups of beer. Were open containers legal in this town?

"Hemingway got soused here every afternoon after writing." The cabbie pointed to a shabby-looking bar, drinkers spilling out onto the sidewalk. "And Jimmy Buffet wrote "A Woman Goin' Crazy on Caroline Street" right down there in Margaritaville." He pointed to yet another bar, lit by palm trees and flamingos in flashing neon, also crammed with boozers.

The whole scene was a police officer's nightmare.

The cab driver swerved onto Caroline Street and pulled over in front of *Notre Paradis*, the bed-and breakfast that Meigs's sister had chosen for him. A thin man wearing a tight white shirt and copper sparkles on his glasses bounded off the front porch to greet him.

"I'm Laurent, your host. This is your first trip to Key West? You're going to love it!" He struck a theatrical pose, and then paused to look Meigs over – his khakis with the worn cuffs and pockets, the gray turtleneck on which he'd spilled his coke during the turbulence from Miami to Key West. Laurent lowered his voice to a whisper and winked. "Yes, there is a lot of money in this town. But there's plenty to enjoy without piles of cash, too."

After unpacking, Meigs changed his shirt and walked up to explore Duval Street on foot. Laurent had dismissed his protests and insisted this was a must-see; had actually escorted him down Caroline Street and watched like a mother seeing her first-born off to kindergarten until Meigs turned to salute goodbye.

On Duval, Meigs stepped over two bums stretched out on cardboard in front of an empty storefront and skirted another playing bad guitar next to a dog dressed in sunglasses and Mardi Gras beads. Every few minutes the dog lifted his snout and howled along with his owner. A handful of tourists stopped to take photos.

"Cruelty to animals," Meigs muttered to himself. Neither the cops nor the residents in his small Connecticut town would have tolerated sleeping bums and singing dogs.

In front of Fast Buck Freddie's tropical window displays, a petite woman in a lime green tube top and a heavyset man with a florid complexion were going at it in hissed whispers. Meigs couldn't help catching "give me some space" followed by "but I paid for the god-damn cruise." Then the big man grabbed the girl's wrist and started to yank her across the sidewalk.

Meigs moved forward and grasped the man's bicep. "Let the lady go," he said in his fiercest cop voice. "Now."

"Fuck off, asshole, this is none of your business," the man said, but dropped his girlfriend's wrist and gave her an unnecessary push.

Meigs turned to her. "Everything okay here? Should I find a policeman?" If he *could* find a cop – so far he'd seen no sign of any law enforcement at all.

"I'm fine," she said, rubbing her wrist and then straightening her sunglasses. She turned to her friend and smiled tremulously. "I will see you later on the ship, George." She disappeared into the stream of shoppers entering Fast Buck Freddie's. The man scowled at Meigs and stalked off in the other direction.

Meigs blew out a breath and left Duval Street – so far the charm of the place was eluding him. He ambled over to the Sunset Celebration at Mallory Square – also mandatory in his host Laurent's mind. He slunk through a bevy of aggressive street performers with minimal musical talent, fended off a tarot card reading, and stopped by a crowd gathered around a slender man in ballet slippers and silver curls who directed a posse of mangy cats. Alice would have found this performance charming. But when the cat man motioned to Meigs to step into the arena to hold a flaming hoop, he fled.

The *Disney Magic*, a ten-story cruise ship decorated with white mouse ears on red smokestacks, was docked on the square. Meigs strode past her and on down the pier to a row of magnificent boats – racing sailboats with names like *Primal Scream* and *Big Booty*. More like big money, Meigs thought. Streams of spectators ogled the boats and their passengers. The largest yacht at the end of the line, the *Emelina*, got the most attention. On its upper deck, a four-man band banged out Buffet tunes for a group of elegant partygoers sipping fizzy drinks in glass flutes.

Meigs sat on a bench for a minute to watch the show. If he was ever worth a couple of million – a billion even – would he moor his ostentatious transportation steps from Mallory Square for every sun-sick passerby to moon over? No, he would not.

Voices floated across the water. "Why don't they move that stinkin' tub so we can see the sunset?" asked a handsome man from the rail of the party boat. He stabbed a finger at the enormous cruise ship across the water and frowned.

"Isn't it illegal to keep a cruise ship at the dock this late?" asked a woman with silver-lacquered nails and matching hair. A flash of sun glinted off the jewels in her belly button.

After the sun set to a smattering of applause, Meigs headed back toward Mallory Square. He stopped at a trolley bar for a Budweiser and leaned against the railing in front of the cruise ship. To his right, the cat man still pranced toe-heel like a misshapen ballerina, calling to the felines in falsetto French, now forcing a yellow tiger to leap over a scrawny black specimen and then through the flaming ring. The tipsy crowd gathered around him howled with appreciation.

Meigs watched the jumpsuited crew of the hulking *Disney Magic* prepare to launch, spooling enormous hanks of steel off cleats on the pier. Why had they been allowed to partially obscure the sunset – the ostensible excuse for this sideshow? Laurent at *Notre Paradis* had assured him this was rule number one on Bone Island (AKA Key West): No boat shall be allowed to obstruct the tourists' view as the sun sinks into the harbor. And its corollary: Tourists must and shall be encouraged to spot the green flash, said by Jules Verne to confer the power to read minds. Meigs doubted the minds here were worth the effort.

A heavy man with a bad sunburn and a loud flowered shirt tenting his gut paced down the gangway that opened from the belly of the ship, out onto the pier, and back. Meigs stiffened, recognizing him as the man he'd seen arguing on Duval Street earlier this afternoon. Two crewmembers dressed in cruise ship whites approached him, but he shrugged off the hand of the taller man, who'd reached out to pat his shoulder. The heavy fellow began to shout and wave his hands but Meigs couldn't make out the words.

"Looks like one of the passengers forgot when their rig was setting sail," said a man next to him. Meigs turned to look him over – he seemed normal enough – blue golf shirt, sunglasses, a beer.

"Will they wait?" Meigs asked.

"Not for long," the man said. "They're fined for leaving late. And the docking fees for cruise ships are prohibitive to begin with."

Meigs watched the three men continue their heated discussion, until finally the heavyset man disappeared into the hull of the ship. He emerged soon after, a porter tailing him with two suitcases, one brown leather, the other faded red denim with yarn flowers wired to the handle. The porter dumped the luggage on the dock and waited a minute for a tip, which was not forthcoming. The crewmen signaled to the workers manning the ropes and the gangway was drawn up. The heavy man steamed up the pier with the luggage, sweating and cursing, and disappeared into the crowd.

"There ees a man who has carried few bags in hees life," said the cat man to Meigs, as he packed his animals into small cages. Meigs nodded, surprised to hear him break character.

The *Disney Magic* pulled away from the dock and Meigs went off in search of a carryout dinner. He refused to sit alone at a table for two at a café on Duval Street where every tourist who passed could feel sorry for him.

~~~

Next morning, Meigs carried his coffee and cereal out to the deck behind his lodging. He skimmed the front page of the *Key West Citizen*, loaded with typical small town stuff – a push to recycle, a scooter/delivery truck crash, projected budget cuts in education and the police department. This last bit of prudence, Meigs thought, would be a false and costly economy. A small town populated by more bars per square inch than New York or New Orleans and a slew of transients and tourists made for barely contained chaos. They needed all the police officers they could hire.

He turned the page and perused the weather forecast – nothing but sunshine and super-humidity for the remainder of his stay. Could he possibly get out a day early? His eye caught on a small article in the crime report at the bottom of the page.

Woman Reported Missing from Cruise Ship, the headline read. As Meigs studied the photograph accompanying the article, his fingers tingled. The clothes were different – a white shirt instead of the green tube top, the hair and make-up more formally styled – but he recognized the picture of the young woman he'd seen arguing with her friend yesterday. According to the paper, the girl's mother had reported her missing, and her travel companion confirmed the disappearance.

He took out his cell phone and dialed the police department's number, but got a busy signal. He wondered if their lines were getting flooded with imagined sightings. In the end, rather than being taken for another attention-seeking fruitcake, he rented a ridiculous, souped-up, open-air golf cart to make the three-mile trek to the KWPD. In person, with a badge in hand, he would be taken seriously. Besides, he'd a lot rather kill time shooting the shit with cops than riding the Conch Tour Train or listening to female impersonators at the La Te Da Cabaret, both of which had been earnestly recommended by his lodging host this morning.

The police station was painted in muted pinks and greens and surrounded by a forest of palm trees. Meigs strode in and introduced himself.

"I'm a detective visiting from Connecticut," he told the officer at the front desk. "I may have some information on the missing person reported in today's newspaper. I'll speak to your chief if he's available."

Minutes later, an attractive man with a wide grin that showcased his even, white teeth against a deep tan emerged from the back and ushered Meigs into his office.

"I'm Chief Ron Barnes." He squeezed Meigs's hand, then sat behind his desk – a lot neater than Meigs kept his – and motioned to the chair in front. "Welcome to Paradise."

"Thanks. I guess." Meigs grunted and pulled the newspaper out of his back pocket. He laid it on the polished desktop and tapped the photo. "The paper said you're looking for this woman?"

"Sort of," said the chief. "This being Key West, we see more than our share of missing persons. Mostly they surface after they've slept off the booze or woken up in some stranger's pad. But Sheila Brown's mother wasn't satisfied with that explanation." He grimaced. "You have information?"

Meigs explained how he'd seen the woman on Duval Street yesterday, filling in as many details of the argument with her boyfriend as he could remember. "When that monster Disney cruise ship was leaving the dock, it looked as though someone was about to miss the boat. Her boyfriend – I'm assuming it's the same man – appeared quite distressed – or gave a good show of it, anyway. He ended up taking some luggage off the big boat and that's the last I saw of either of them."

"George Vesper – the boyfriend – is coming in to touch base shortly," said the chief. "You're welcome watch the interview from our observation room if you're interested."

Meigs was. A sergeant installed him behind a one-way mirror and soon after, ushered Vesper into the room with the chief. Dressed in sharply-creased khakis, a blue silk shirt, and an expensive-looking watch, Vesper appeared less disheveled than he had yesterday on the dock, but even more sour. Chief Barnes asked him to recount the facts of yesterday's disappearance.

"Sheila wanted to check out the shops on Duval Street," Vesper said. "And when a gal wants to shop, I stay out of her way." He shook his head and grinned. "I'm not one of those pantywaist dopes who tags along to sit outside the dressing room and approve every damn purchase. I gave her a couple hundred bucks and told her to knock her lovely self out. This trip with Sheila wasn't going to be cheap," – he waggled his carefully groomed eyebrows – "but worth it, if you know what I mean."

"Were you and Ms. Brown experiencing problems with your relationship?"

Meigs noticed the muscles in Vesper's neck tighten. The thin hank of hair that had been combed across his sunburned pate trembled. He patted it down and frowned at the chief. "Not at all. She's a delightful girl and the trip has been great so far."

The chief settled his elbows on the table and leaned forward. "What's your theory about her disappearance, Mr. Vesper?"

Vesper pursed his lips, the overhead fluorescents casting sallow shadows under his eyes. "Maybe she met an old friend and tied one on. I expect she'll show up later today. Frankly, her mother's a worrywart – it's a shame to squander your department's resources on this."

"Let's take down some basic information, as long as you're here," said Chief Barnes. He opened up the small computer on the table in front of him. "Let's start with you."

Vesper reported that he was a businessman from Connecticut, age 54, and this was his first cruise on the Disney line. He had been dating Ms. Brown for five months. They'd met in a local Mexican restaurant on half-price margarita night – she was a server in the cocktail lounge. Vesper owned four furniture stores along the Connecticut shoreline, and no, they did not carry crappy fiberboard pieces like the ones advertised by that buffoon on television. His outfit focused on high-quality wood and styles consistent with old New England fashion. He was divorced, two kids from a previous marriage that he seldom saw, even though he'd paid through the goddamned nose for prep school and college tuition.

"What about Sheila?" said Barnes, looking up from the keyboard. "What's her background?"

Vesper hesitated, patted his forehead with a neatly folded handkerchief. Despite their relatively short acquaintance, he said, he'd been swept away both by her physical presence and her personality. "A live wire with a very soft spot for a middle-aged man," was how he described her.

"Maybe she had a daddy complex and maybe she didn't," added Vesper. "I can tell you that what went on between us was not parental."

Meigs rolled his eyes. What had Miss Brown seen in this bozo?

Chief Barnes asked for contact information on the missing girl, but Vesper was vague. He hadn't met any of her relatives, though she had made nightly calls to her mother, often in his presence. And she lived with a roommate – another waitress – when she wasn't staying with him. Vesper had already called her but the friend claimed she hadn't heard from Sheila since they'd left Connecticut. He paged through his iPhone and found the friend's phone number.

"You're wasting your time though," he said after reading it off.

Behind the mirror, Meigs jotted the number on his newspaper.

"Call us if you think of anything else. Were you traveling with friends?"

"Just us." Vesper refolded the handkerchief and stuffed it into his pocket. "I'm staying at the Marquesa Hotel. You can reach me there or on my cell." He shook hands with Barnes and left the room.

"He's got some dough," said Chief Barnes, once Meigs was back in the conference room and the door clicked shut behind him. "No one stays at the Marquesa unless they're rich, famous, or both. What's your impression?"

"He's a liar," said Meigs.

Chief Barnes looked startled.

Meigs repeated how he'd seen Vesper and the girlfriend arguing on Duval Street, how she'd wanted some time alone. "So the trip *wasn't* going well and he *is* the kind of pantywaist dope who wants to tag along shopping."

Chief Barnes laughed. "What else?"

"Most of the cruise ship disappearances I've heard about ended up with one of the parties murdered," Meigs added. "Didn't Vesper sound as though he didn't want you looking too hard for her?" Meigs tapped his fingers on the table. "But chances are, she got tired of this clown and bailed out. I imagine that cruise ship cabin could have felt awfully small after a few nights entertaining Vesper."

The chief laughed again. "You 're right about that. I'll put one of my guys on it, ask around at Sunset tonight to see if anyone else saw her or talked to her. Thanks for stopping in," he added. "As you probably read in the *Citizen* this morning, the sailboat races are in town and we're stretched thin."

"I'd be happy to do some research," Meigs offered.

"We'll be fine," said the chief, his voice cool now.

Meigs motored back into town and stopped at the pink cement library on Fleming Street. He couldn't help himself – and what were the options? Alice would have wanted to tour Hemingway's house, have her picture taken at the Southernmost Point, order pina coladas and watch the human interest show from a streetside bar on Duval. Dismal prospects without her.

Meigs settled at one of the computers in between a teenage girl with multiple eyebrow piercings and a shabby man whose odor suggested he hadn't put soap to skin in some time. He started by Googling George Vesper. As Vesper had boasted, his four furniture businesses appeared to be doing well. Very well. An article in *Fortune Small Business* dissected his success and reduced it to customer service, quality manufacturing, and an aggressive marketing campaign that targeted wealthy homeowners along the Connecticut shoreline. For the article, Vesper had been photographed at his own waterfront home in Greenwich, which Meigs figured had to be worth eight or ten million. He also owned a "cottage" on Nantucket and a thirty-five foot sailboat moored at a fashionable and pricy Cos Cob marina. During his limited down time, Vesper enjoyed competing in local regattas. He appeared to have plenty of money and no problem flaunting it.

Next Meigs Googled Sheila Brown and skimmed dozens of links about Sheila the artist, Sheila the fifth grade teacher, Sheila the lawyer, Sheila the nature photographer. But nothing about Sheila the waitress.

Meigs then typed the Disney cruise ship's name into the search bar. The *Disney Magic* was a mid-priced boat offering a standard Western Caribbean winter break itinerary, including

Key West, Cozumel, Grand Cayman, and Castaway Cay. He sat back in his chair, trying to ignore the homeless man next to him muttering as he rustled through a filthy knapsack. Meigs could definitely imagine Vesper steering by his genitals. But why on earth would a man with his alleged assets and sailing expertise choose a floating Disney city loaded with middle-class folks and their offspring? *Disney*, for god's sake. The girlfriend must have chosen it.

He logged out of the computer and returned to his B and B. Back on the deck, Meigs called the number of Sheila Brown's waitress friend and roommate, Maya Redkin.

"This is Detective Jack Meigs, on behalf of the Key West Police Department." So it was a little stretcher – she'd never check on him. He explained about Sheila's disappearance and her boyfriend's worry.

"I haven't heard a peep since she left," Maya protested. "Oh my gosh, did something happen to her?

"That's under investigation," said Meigs, noting that not getting involved came before concern, for Sheila's alleged best friend. "She left the ship to do some shopping yesterday and didn't return. How would you characterize her relationship with George Vesper?"

There was a long pause. "He treated her well. Took her out to expensive restaurants and clubs. Bought her some nice stuff and sent some gorgeous flowers. Apparently he's loaded. What's not to like about that?"

"Would you say they were serious? In love? Was marriage in their future?"

Maya laughed. "Now that would surprise me, especially since she has another boyfriend." She stopped and corrected herself: "Had one. And isn't Vesper a little old for her?"

"That would be her decision," said Meigs, bristling silently. He was the same age as Vesper, without the big belly and the big bucks. Not that he wanted a girlfriend half his age, but was he over the hill too? "What about other family members? Friends? Anyone I can call who might know where she is?"

"She kept those numbers on her cell phone," said Maya.

"Was it Sheila who chose the cruise?"

"He planned everything – he liked to control things, you know? Listen, I have to get to work."

"Call us if you hear from her," said Meigs. "Save us a lot of trouble."

"Wait. What's the weather like down there?" Maya asked in a wistful voice. "It's ten degrees here and snowing."

"Incessantly sunny."

Meigs signed off and leaned back in his rocker. The roommate was definitely not concerned about Sheila. Nor was she impressed with the solidity of her relationship with Vesper. Both of which pointed to the likelihood that Sheila had fled rather than been taken by force. He let his thoughts wander to Vesper, his business in Connecticut, his flamboyant wealth. And this brought to mind a Connecticut entrepreneur who'd allowed his wealth to taint his judgment: Stew Leonard. Leonard had siphoned off cash from his high-end grocery shops in the 1990's with a sophisticated software scam and then served jail time for tax fraud.

Meigs grabbed his hat and sunglasses and hurried back to the pier at Mallory Square. A Carnival cruise ship had taken the place of the *Disney Magic* and the cat man was setting up for the evening's performance.

"I'd like to buy one of your t-shirts," said Meigs. He pointed to a light-blue shirt with "The cat man and his flying house cats" written across the chest. When he'd paid for the shirt, he showed his badge and handed him the newspaper photo of Sheila. "This woman disappeared yesterday and I'm wondering if you happened to see her."

The cat man studied it and gave it back. "I can't be certain, they pass through here like herds of mutton."

"But maybe..." Meigs said.

"Eet was almost dark, but maybe she boarded the beeg yacht at the end of the pier." He pointed to the empty slip that yesterday had held the *Emelina*. "After the cruise sheep was gone."

Meigs thanked him, trotted back to *Notre Paradis*, and asked to use Laurent's computer. He Googled the Emelina. One hundred and sixty-seven feet long, the boat had been sold in Monaco and was expected to winter in St. Bart's. He jotted down the owner's information and tucked it into his pocket, then started off for the Marquesa Hotel. A chat with George Vesper was in order.

The Marquesa's lobby was caviar to Meigs's hotel's scrambled eggs. The soft hiss of a waterfall and the rustling of the uplighted palm fronds masked the scooter traffic outside. Vesper was splayed in a chaise near the poolside bar. He beckoned over a server dressed in blue Bermuda shorts and ordered a super single malt bourbon that Meigs had never heard of.

"Mr. Vesper?"

The man glanced up, his face blank.

"I'm Detective Meigs, Guilford Police Department. Following up on the reported disappearance of Sheila Brown."

Vesper pinched his lips together in a tight frown and said nothing. Meigs couldn't tell if he recognized him from the altercation on Duval Street. If he did, he wasn't acknowledging their connection.

"Do you happen to know the owner or the crew of the Emelina? That's one of the yachts that were moored a nine-iron from your cruise ship yesterday."

The waiter approached and settled a drink on the glass table next to Vesper. Vesper didn't even look at the man, never mind thank or tip him.

"Can't say that I do," Vesper answered, taking a swallow of the gold liquid. "What does that have to do with Sheila?"

"Any chance that she would have had friends on that boat?"

"Sheila?" Vesper threw back his head and roared with laughter. "That girl lived from tip to tip. No way she'd have pals that wealthy." Then he sat up and scowled. "Why do you ask?"

"Might she have been connected with one of the crew members? Maybe cadged a ride out of town?"

Vesper's face turned from red to purple. "If that no-good bastard boyfriend..." He chugged the rest of the drink as he scrambled to his feet, now hulking over Meigs.

"Was anything missing from your cabin after Sheila went shopping?" Meigs persisted.

Vesper took off his glasses and glared. "Look, this has all been a big mistake. I should have told you right up front. We had an awful row that morning and she said she was taking the first plane home. Which was fine with me, only she took my ruby ring and the cash in my wallet, too."

"I'm sure Chief Barnes can radio the coast guard, have a chat with the captain and see whether Sheila's on board. Insist she return your belongings."

"Never mind that," Vesper growled. "I can take it from here. I'll settle this with her at home."

"As you like," said Meigs, starting back toward the lobby. "I'll fill in the chief. He may wish to follow up. I would imagine the IRS might have some questions too."

"This is none of your damn business," Vesper sputtered after him. "What's a Connecticut cop doing working a Key West case anyway?"

Meigs left the Marquesa, loaded back into his golf cart, and returned to the police station and asked to speak to the chief.

"I came across some information on that missing persons case," he said to Chief Barnes. "If you contact the pilot of the Emelina yacht, I suspect you'll find that Sheila Brown stowed aboard with a large sum of cash. The cash may have come courtesy of cooking the books at Vesper's furniture business. It's kind of a tradition in Connecticut." He smiled. "Stew Leonard, Martha Stewart, even former Governor John Rowland. Some of the wealthy folks in our state aren't quite satisfied with what they've got. So they stretch the rules to suit them."

"That's an awfully big leap," said the chief.

"Not really," said Meigs. "Vesper just didn't seem like a cruise ship kind of guy. And the magic of Disney? I don't think so. Then I noticed the Grand Cayman Island was included on the itinerary. Suppose Vesper had made substantial illegal gains and intended to bank the money offshore. The Disney cruise would be a terrific cover. But his companion figured this out and disappeared with his cash. No wonder he was upset."

Chief Barnes shook his head. "That's a hell of a lotta supposition."

"Your cat man saw Sheila stow aboard the Emelina after sunset," said Meigs. "While he's working his felines, he watches everything."

On the way home from the police station, Meigs stopped at The Lost Weekend package store for a six-pack of Red Stripe beer. Back in his room, he changed into his cat man t-shirt and took a beer out onto the back deck.

Maybe this vacation thing wasn't so bad after all. Maybe tomorrow he'd buy a ticket for the Conch Train and another for a tour of the Little White House, in memory of Alice.

~~~

Four days later, as Meigs finished packing for home, Chief Barnes texted him.

Coast Guard located the Emelina in the British Virgin Islands. Sheila and bf onboard with 3 hundred K cash. Thx 4 the assist.

Meigs texted back *ur welcome.*

Then he called the taxi company for a ride to airport, specifically requesting a bird-free cab. Still, he wasn't surprised when a golden retriever the size of a donkey lumbered out of the van's passenger seat and began to sniff his luggage.

"Don't you even think of it," he shouted.

4. Four Fingers and the Dead Drag Queen

Shirrel Rhoades

Wharton "Four Fingers" Dalessandro hoisted the bottle of Red Stripe and chugalugged it. He was ready to go home to his cigar-maker's cottage on Olivia Street after an evening at the Schooner Wharf with his pal Dunk Reid. It wasn't hard to outdrink the diminutive islander, for at 5' 10" Four Fingers had a lot more body mass to absorb the alcohol than Dunk. Like a wizen leprechaun, Dunk would be lucky to hit 5' 2" in his stocking feet.

Not that the little man ever wore stockings, for the summer weather in Key West was just too hot, even with the sea breezes. Like most people who lived here, he wore boat shoes with no socks, baggy Bermuda shorts, and a colorful T-shirt. Today's tee offered A PENNY FOR YOUR THOUGHTS. A DOLLAR IF YOU FLASH ME!

Forget about the dollar. With New Year's Eve coming up, girls would unhesitatingly flash you for 10¢ worth of plastic beads.

Welcoming in the New Year was a big deal on Duval Street. Every year at the Bourbon Street Pub a drag queen known as

Sushi dropped at midnight in a giant papier-mâché slipper, spewing sparkling champagne from a bottle onto the cheering crowds. Guys in the hoard below were bare-chested, or wore chaps with buttocks showing, or displayed more tats that Ray Bradbury's Illustrated Man. The women were mostly blonde, sometimes with cowboy hats, necks laden with strands of cheap plastic beads, raising their T-shirts and blouses to display their boobs in return for more wampum.

Anderson Cooper and Kathy Griffith would cut from Times Square to Key West to check out what outrageous things Sushi might say this year. Like the time she stated that "Anderson Cooper is out and about," but the scene clicked off at "Anderson Cooper is out ..." That was before the silver-haired commentator officially came out of the closet. Sushi took a little heat for that, not that it bothered her.

Dunk and Four Fingers usually spent their New Year's on the other side of the island, at the Bight where the Schooner Wharf Bar lowered a pirate wench at midnight. Yo ho ho.

Not that they didn't enjoy Sushi's outrageous antics, but there was a loyalty owed to the Schooner Wharf because the proprietors let them play chess on the premises every afternoon. After the chess game, the guys might linger for a bite of dinner, maybe even enjoy a few bottles of beer. After all this time at the bar they knew the words to entertainer Michael McCloud's songs better than he did.

McCloud was the island's answer to Jimmy Buffett, who had abandoned Key West after becoming famous, leaving his Margaritaville bar behind as a memento. McCloud was famous for writing the Conch Republic National Anthem, a paean to leaving northern cold weather behind. The Conch Republic is another name for Key West, a holdover from those drug-running days when bales of square grouper (i.e. marijuana) floated ashore nightly.

That was long before Four Fingers came to Key West to embrace a sedate existence as a sometimes housepainter, after twenty years as a homicide dick with the NYPD. He'd been down here seventeen years, but still couldn't get over the fact that he was now living in Paradise.

His pal Dunk was a true Key Wester, the man's family going back five generations on the island. That made him a Conch (pronounced "konk"), a status only birth could bestow. Dunk's father had been a burly man who once arm-wrestled Ernest Hemingway and fished for giant marlin with the great writer back in the '30s. Right after that Hemingway became a war correspondent, derisively called "Ernie Hemorrhoid," a play on the name of that other great contemporary journalist, Ernie Pyle. After that, Hemingway migrated to Cuba with his new lady friend, leaving his Key West compound to become a tourist attraction.

Being a Conch, Dunk Reid had more relatives than Biblical Adam. He was always introducing people as "my cousin" to Four Fingers. That's why tonight while Four Fingers chugalugged his last beer before heading home, he didn't think much about the man who slipped onto a barstool next to him. The gaunt scarecrow had been introduced to him as "Cousin Raf."

Raf – short for Rafael – was Dunk's mother's sister's boy, a 38-year-old ne'er-do-well who sometimes worked as a shrimper. An uncut shock of sandy hair made his narrow face appear even slimmer. His clothes looked dirty, his unwashed feet encased in untied boat shoes. He held up a Marlboro, a cig he'd obviously bummed off someone.

"Got a light, man?"

"Don't smoke," replied Four Fingers. "But that cigar roller over there will let you use his torch." A dark-haired Cuban set up shop every night at Schooner Wharf, rolling cigars made with "100% Cuban-seed tobacco."

"Can you lend me twenty dollars?"

Four Fingers grunted a *no*. "Ask your cousin over here," he nodded toward Dunk, who was all but head-on-the-bar drunk.

"No way," mumbled Dunk, shooing away the request with a wave of his free hand; the other one clutching a Budweiser. "Raf still owes me ten dollars from last week."

"Hey, I'll pay you back outta the twenty."

"Oh, okay," hiccupped Dunk. Four Fingers rolled his eyes as the inebriated little man peeled off a twenty from his roll and handed it to his cousin. "Now gimme my ten," demanded Dunk.

"You got change?"

"Sure, here." Dunk passed him two tens and the man handed one back – now in possession of the original twenty plus the ten.

"Thanks, cousin," said Raf.

"Don't mention it."

Four Fingers was pretty sure Raf wouldn't mention it, hoping that Dunk was too drunk to remember the exchange. "I'm heading home," he said, sliding his butt off the barstool. The sand under his feet seemed a little unsteady.

"Fore you go, wanna see a dead man?"

He turned to the slender man. "Who's dead?" The old cop juices bubbling in his brain.

"Dunno. Some tourist I think. Gilded Glenda showed him to me a few minutes ago. Out there in the back alley behind the bandstand."

Gilded Glenda (née Harvey Milnik) was a drag queen known for her penchant for gold lamé gowns. She worked her way from bar to bar, dancing for tourists in return for drinks – the later the evening, the wilder her terpsichorean antics.

"Better show me," said Four Fingers.

"Cost you twenty dollars."

Without hesitating, Four Fingers forked over the portrait of Alexander Hamilton. "Let's go see the dead man."

Raf led him and Dunk to the back of the bar, a dusty street barely wide enough for a beer delivery truck. Tonight it was clogged with parked cars – two rusty Jeeps, an old VW, a Ford with a cracked windshield, and a shiny Hummer. "Dead guy's in that Hummer. Pecked on his window to borrow a dollar for a beer when I noticed he had a big ol' knife sticking in his chest."

"Where does Gilded Glenda come in?"

"Oh, she was sitting in the Hummer beside the dead man. Man, her makeup was a mess. Mascara running down her cheeks. Hair looked like a bird's nest."

"Where's Glenda now?"

"Who knows? She bolted when she saw me at the window. Jumped out of that big-ass vehicle an' run like a ghost was chasing her."

Four Fingers walked around to the driver's side, peered in the open window. Sure enough, a slender knife like you use to filet fish was protruding awkwardly from the man's chest. Eyes closed, mouth open, his face had achieved a pale yellowish cast in death. He wore an expensive Tommy Bahama shirt, pressed slacks with unzipped fly, Nike running shoes. An open red-and-white pack of Marlboros was balanced on the tan dashboard above the steering wheel. The registration in the glove box identified him as Roger Allen Willard of Valdosta, Georgia. The Hummer bore that out with a Georgia license plate.

"Yep, looks like a tourist all right. Johnny Leigh's not going to be very happy about this." The police chief's main imperative was to prevent visitors from getting harmed – tourism being the backbone of the island's economy. Under Chief Leigh's so-far eight-year term, murders had declined 27%. Petty burglaries were up 4%, but no one cared about that.

"Hey, I'm not hanging around for the police. I'll bid you gentlemen goodnight. You two can play Good Citizen and call it in. Just don't mention my name."

"Can't do that," said Four Fingers.

"Why not?"

"'Cause you killed ol' Roger Willard here. Gilded Glenda will confirm that when we find her."

"Well, then I'm walking, cause you ain't gonna find that crossdressing bitch. She's gone for good."

"Oh? Where did you put her body?"

"Huh?"

"Here's what happened: Glenda was giving this tourist a blowjob in his Hummer – no pun intended. His fly's open. You came along and stabbed him for his fat wallet, then offed Glenda because she witnessed the whole thing."

"No, it happened like I told you."

"Couldn't have. You said you knocked on the window, but as you can see it's open. A dead man couldn't have rolled it down."

"Maybe Gilded Glenda rolled it down."

"You said she bolted. No time to fiddle with the window. Glenda's nervous and high-strung; she wouldn't have been sitting here in this vehicle alone with a dead man. She only ran when you stabbed her john."

"How d'you know *she* didn't put the knife in him?" Raf was looking panicky, like he was about to cut and run. But Dunk held onto his arm, a flimsy restrain given the little man's inebriated condition.

"By its angle in his chest. He was stabbed through the open window."

"Damn. Guess I may as well admit it. Glenda's dead too. She grabbed the man's wallet as she rabbited. So I had to chase her down to get it. That wallet was rightfully mine after I kilt the guy. She put up a fight; hit me with one of her spiked heels. You oughta see the bruise on my chest. So I hit her back with a brick. You'll find her over there where the trailer park used to be."

Dunk looked over the top of his eyeglasses as if studying a bug. "If you stole the man's wallet, why were you hitting me up for ten dollars? You oughta been buying me drinks instead."

Raf lowered his eyes, embarrassed by the failure of his criminal endeavor. "The damn wallet was empty. Guy didn't have a cent on him. He was gonna stiff Glenda for that blowjob, so he deserved everything he got."

Four Fingers wagged his head at Raf's convoluted logic. But, in his experience, criminals were not the smartest people on earth. "Another dead giveaway – no pun. You were looking for a light for a Marlboro. And there's an open pack in the Hummer with one cig missing. You didn't just steal his wallet, you stole a cigarette too."

"Hell, he wasn't gonna smoke it now, was he?"

"One other thing I'm curious about. Why did you tell us about the dead man in the first place? If you'd simply walked away and kept your mouth shut, you might never have been caught."

"Simple. The wallet was empty an' I needed some money. You paid me twenty dollars to show him to you."

"That twenty dollars is going to cost you twenty years – or worse."

"Worse? You mean Old Sparky? No jury in this town's gonna give me a death sentence. I've got too many relatives here. Right, Dunk?"

Raf's cousin shook his head, a grim look on his face as if he'd just sucked on a lime. "Not sure even the Bubba network can save you this time."

Four Fingers pulled his battered Nokia from his pocket. "Hold on while I call Johnny Leigh," he said, dialing the number with his left hand. That missing index finger on his right paw made using a cellphone tricky.

"Sure, take your time. I'm in no hurry to go to Raiford." That's Florida's notorious state prison where Old Sparky resides, although lethal injection is the most common form of execution at FSP these days.

"Raf, you done acted the fool one too many times," said Dunk, starting to sober up. "What am I gonna tell your sainted mama?"

"That she shoulda give me a trust fund like you got. Otherwise, I wouldn't have killed two people over an empty wallet."

"That's your only regret?" asked Dunk. "An empty wallet?"

"No, one other thing."

"What's that?"

"Too bad about Glenda," said Dunk's cousin. "I always had a thing for that gal."

5. Saving Gloria

Jessica Argyle

"I used to be snow white – but I drifted."

-Mae West

He was there, listening, when the gavel came down for Gloria.

"Ten Years." Raymond held his breath. "Suspended."

Mrs. Smail, her parole officer, claimed that Gloria's incredible good fortune was a combination of luck and planning. Raymond's offer of employment helped, as did her otherwise clean record. And Gloria was lucky, the judge she drew was known for his strong belief in salvation.

Raymond had never seen her high, and had difficulty imagining what she would be like. Anyone can make a mistake, but not in Florida. Florida's drug laws are among the harshest in the country. Everyone knew about them. Everyone, apparently, but Gloria.

Mrs. Smail's own son was incarcerated, which explained her grim view of human nature. It had probably been years since she had seen a happy ending. Mrs. Smail understood that Raymond had mixed motives but took him at his word when he offered Gloria a job at his plant nursery. When she asked him why he wanted to help Gloria, he said, "She has a natural aptitude for design and is a willing student."

If only that were true, he thought as he signed the affidavit to the board.

He was happily surprised when Gloria took to the nursery, read books on plant propagation, orchid culture.

While she was working, he was working out and even considered getting his hair thickened somehow, but Gloria seemed to like him just as he was. One evening when he arrived for the day's receipts, she and Octavio, Key West's reigning orchid king, were pairing Catteleyas with Paphs.

She was laughing, flirting with him, saying, "Don't you think they look great together. The paphs look like villains and the cats are frilly, bright, girly."

Raymond couldn't believe that orchid-obsessed Octavio, allowed this. Even Raymond knew that the two species had completely different light requirements.

"Don't they make a handsome couple," Gloria said, smiling manically, pointing to a couple of plants, and in spite of his irritation, Raymond was charmed by her.

Later that week, Mrs. Smail snuck up on them, coming through the back door of the shop and he with his palm up Gloria's broomstick skirt.

"I think she's jealous."

"No, just protective. She wants to save me."

Soon the shop became Mrs. Smail's favorite spot to drop in on Gloria. Tired of hiding, after the first six months Raymond took a deep breath and asked her to move in with him but quickly he realized that marrying her might be her true salvation, so he bought the ring and married her in a ceremony on the beach, one in which Mrs. Smail was notably absent. Octavio made Gloria a crown of orchids, offering it to her, saying, "Paphs and cats, together at last."

But marrying Gloria was not the tonic he had thought it would be. He cut her hours at the shop so she could oversee the renovation on the large house they purchased in Key West near the beach. But she thought everyone was taking them for money and soon the workers made excuses not to come. Simple jobs took twice as along as they should have and Gloria moved around the house with a heavy gait, weighted eyes. She threw a tantrum when the hurricane windows didn't fit properly and Raymond had to stop her from picking at the skin around her nails.

"Calm down, Mrs. Smail is due this afternoon. I don't know why you can't meet her at a restaurant or something? I hate that she snoops around here like she's looking to catch you at something."

"You knew what you were in for. I have years of probation left. This *is* Florida." Her eyes took on that slightly veiled look whenever she spoke about jail time.

So Raymond put up with it convinced that Mrs. Smail (he refused to call her Barbara) engineered situations where she could stand next to him, being a good three or four inches taller.

When he walked into the kitchen they were there, the two of them, making coffee, Gloria cool, secretive as if the hysterics had never happened.

"Maybe you should get back to work," he suggested after Mrs. Smail left. "You seem annoyed lately, unhappy." She had started to cook, vegan, and he didn't know what was worse, the legless mush or the sharp pains afterward. When he worked up the nerve to complain, she told him to make his own dinner.

"I'd like to introduce you to something really amazing," she said later that evening, "The twenty-first century."

She wore white leggings and a semi-sheer knit top that shimmered when she spoke. She glistened all the way to the door and tossed him a hot pink smile before she disappeared.

Although it was another sweltering day in Key West, Raymond felt cold and dry. He had waited until he was fifty-nine years old to marry, but he now wondered if what he had really wanted to do was save her. She was fascinating to him, mercurial. She used to love it when he called her Snow White because of her dramatic coloring, but now she would make a face, eyes vacuous, mimicking a doll. It turned out the nickname was an irony. How was Ray to know that once she stopped working, she would spend days in the beautiful home like the living dead, lying around in a coma followed by bouts of manic activity? Lately she looked at him in a way that made him aware that he was shorter than she was. It was only an inch but it may as well have been a foot. Inside the first half year of marriage she began to wear heels. Gone were the ballerina flats of the dating days replaced with Manolo Blahnik, Jimmy Choo and Louboutin. All stiletto all the time.

Raymond turned the television on, refusing to allow his blood pressure to rise by getting angry with Snow White. He was pissed though, pissed that her leaving prevented him from enjoying *Dance For Your Life*.

He walked up the long winding staircase to their extravagant bedroom, rummaged around in a drawer and found his XL t-shirt and a pair of loose jogging pants. Who cared what he looked like if there was no one around to criticize? He returned to the couch out of breath and the thought of jogging into the restaurant-sized kitchen just about did him in. But the bag of bite-size brownies and cheesies called to him from their hiding place above the cavernous sink.

He slid on the marble floors in stocking feet, skiing into the kitchen. For a moment, a second, really, he felt the tiniest bit of exhilaration. Foolish and free, he climbed the kitchen ladder, opened the cupboard and felt around for the cheesies. *Jesus, where were they?*

Reaching in and balancing on his tiptoes, he felt the edge of a package. He reached in further, lost his grip and an envelope fell into the deep enameled sink with a dull thud. Something bounced out of the envelope creating a series of pings that echoed through the kitchen.

Three translucent orange bottles lay at the bottom of the sink magnificently crowned with glittery white caps. *Oh no, not this again.* They had three names, three different pharmacies *but what were they?* Seraquil, Vicodin, Hydracodone. *Who the hell was she?* His palms grew clammy when he handled them. *So that's what she's up to. That's what's been happening.* He returned all but one to their hiding place. *Insurance,* he thought. *If Gloria was sneaky enough to hide them from him, she would be sneaky enough to move them.*

When Gloria returned he was half-asleep on the couch. He watched her movements out of the corner of his eye, as she tiptoed around him. He could sense her relief that he wouldn't be joining her in bed. Soundlessly, he watched her with hooded eyes as she took off her shoes and stole up the stairs.

He woke up edgy and disoriented a few hours later.

Her clothes of the previous evening were in the hamper and when he called to her, she yelled, "I'll be out in a minute."

He made his way to the hamper, reached in and grabbed her white leggings, her lacy thong underwear knotted in the legs.

He ran his fingernail over the crotch area, then raised the leggings to his nose.

"Are you kidding me?" She was standing, the door ajar, peeking through the opening.

"What do you expect me to think?

"Jesus, it was just an evening out. You could have joined us." She glared at him, her eyes like scars, and slammed the door shut. He knew exactly how ridiculous he sounded. He checked her phone and saw calls from Mrs. Smail and Jill, *her old friend with the midnight blue dye job. Jesus.*

Humiliated, the deep crease in the folds of flesh at the back of his neck began to perspire. He stood there taking it all in, the room, the shower, all the while holding the thong entwined leggings by the tiny crotch.

Quickly, before she opened the door again, he raised them to his nose and took a deep sniff. *Nothing*, so he wiped his neck with the limp white legging and dropped them back into the hamper.

Gloria emerged wrapped in a horizontally striped towel. Only she could get away with thick brown and green horizontal and still look like Snow White, elegant, creamy. But when she turned away, he felt sorry for her. She smoothed her ragged hair with mutilated nails and tugged at the towel to keep it closed.

The next morning Raymond asked Gloria if she wanted to go for a ride in the car to Miami, maybe stop in Coconut Grove and do some shopping but then he remembered that she had yet another appointment with the PO.

"No worries, said Gloria. She left the job, and they haven't assigned anyone else to me yet," Gloria said.

"But she was only a few years from a full pension." *Am I finally rid of that woman?*

"She doesn't care. She didn't report something," Gloria smiled like she had something to be proud of. "She doesn't like to turn people in, she's lost all respect for the system."

"Does that mean we get to go away for a bit?"

"I'm all yours."

They would talk in the car in neutral territory, away from routine. Before she answered him, the phone rang. "For you," he said tossing her the phone. "Mrs. Smail." He smirked. Oblivious, she phony-smiled at him and took the call in another room.

Coconut Grove was three hours away and they had always liked talking on long car rides. He never tired of the Florida Keys, remained enchanted by the slim shoreline, the fragility of terrain that had yet been here forever. Gloria used to look for iguanas saying, *Don't you find it creepy the way they sort of smile at you?* He found their robotic movements enchanting. Their unnatural emerald green otherworldly beautiful.

Today the sky was too bright, colors surreal, opaque sea glass, sandbars zigzagging into water. Once, when a storm threatened, they drove over the Seven-Mile Bridge into a grainy haze, impossible to decipher sea from sky from land. When they got to the other side, his porcelain girl had the slightest flush and they stopped the car on the side of a dune. They made love hidden in plain sight of traffic intent on escape. And this was how he imagined their life together. They had fled to the end of the world, Key West, where anything seemed possible. *It's easy to be old here,* he thought. Seniors walked around in string bikinis, male and female shapeshifters, asexual as time overtook them. Here old men rode bright pastel bicycles, thin hair blowing away from receding hairlines.

And because he forgot how old he was, he expected her to feel the same. Filled with goodwill, for all that he had to offer his wife, when he turned to look, her eyes were a little like the iguanas, fixed, barren.

"C'mon Gloria, cycling, dancing and then dinner on the waterfront? Shopping first, of course shopping."

"If that's what you want."

The eerie wavering pitch of her voice unnerved him. "I don't shop," he said. "Talk to me. Stop being such a kid."

She seemed about to answer him, but didn't. So he turned on the sports station, loud. Gloria curled up in her seat her nose pressed up against the window. She looked a little like a cat he once tried to tame, eyes fixed on the door, body in a false relaxed position. At once Raymond realized how much she truly longed for release. The closer they got to Miami the darker her spirits seemed to grow. She lit a cigarette in the car without bothering to open the window. Raymond stepped on the gas pedal and when she leaned into the dashboard, he tapped the brakes enough to send her reeling forward then hit the back of her seat hard.

"Who's the juvenile?" She asked him.

"Twenty-eight hardly qualifies you as a juvenile. More your actions.'

"You married me." She flicked her cigarette butt out the window and he thought about the four hundred dollar fine if they were caught. He thought about the bottle of Vicodin in his bag.

Gloria smiled lazily at him as if she enjoyed his discomfort; as if she had come to some sort of decision.

It now dawned on him that she was sneaking medication, had never really stopped. It all began to make sense, the moodiness, the vague look in her eyes. *Does she really have to be medicated just to put up with me?*

The hotel they stopped at in Coconut Grove was pure seventies.

"It's been in the same family for the past thirty-five years," the waitress said, ushering them to the bar. "It's the only building in the area that hasn't been turned into a condo. Sculpted mushroom-colored broadloom and crinkle amber candle holders set this off as a period piece. Once he would have found it charming but now it just made Ray feel old.

"You guys could all be from the same family," Gloria laughed gesturing toward another couple. Raymond tried to smile, nodding in agreement. He maintained an air of calm but was tired of being bullied by her youth.

"You two doin' alright."

They spoke to each other through the waitress.

"You kids need a little sustenance. A little coating to steel yourself for tonight when the drinking really begins around here." She put a maternal hand on Gloria's shoulder and said, "Pretty girl." He could feel the vibration of Gloria's purr.

Raymond enjoyed the generosity of the gesture. It dawned on him that his wife was always being rewarded for a lack of something – experience, ability. He continued making conversation with the waitress, encouraging her diatribe about former plans for the hotel, waning business and why she wore one brand of shoe over another.

"These are comfortable *and* sexy," she said pointing to her orthopedic shoes. She mimicked a model when she returned with their Mojitos, laughing at herself all the while. *Irony*, Raymond thought, *a sense of irony is what's missing*. He laughed with her as she met his eyes.

Gloria looked like a small sparrow, open eyes blinking, and Raymond resented her for having no ability to see beyond the woman's uniform to her athletic movements. He could easily imagine the waitress naked and happy, a willing participant. Gloria's expressions were those of a dutiful daughter along for the ride, tolerant. He should have known that saving Gloria would only make him feel older than his years, not younger.

When Gloria made her way to the bathroom, Raymond deliberately relaxed his shoulders. She returned, composed, friendly, as if she had made a decision to be kind. She moved her drink to his side of the booth and slid in beside him.

"Ray, relax. Let's not fight. I hate it when you look at me like that." Her smile was forced, her eyes focused, slick. She played with her drink, took a sip, puffed up her lips and kissed him softly.

Her eyes were half closed Marilyn-style, dreamy. It was the look she had when he gave her things, when they married, when they first made love that night on the dune. He knew in a terrible instant that they had always been there, the drugs. That's what made her so vague, gave her the ethereal edge that he felt such tenderness for and explained the hardness after. *She must have been coming down then.*

Raymond had a good idea of what had just happened. She had comforted herself by taking something in the bathroom. This had been going on for months, since they met, before, beyond. He felt horrified, sorry for himself.

Seeing as you like it so much, lets make it a triple whammy.

He slid a spoon into his pocket, went into the bathroom, crushed two tablets on a coaster returned and slipped them into her drink.

He checked his watch. The waitress returned with fresh drinks. She leaned over to Gloria and Ray poured the remains of her first drink into the fresh one. "Waste not, want not," he said, causing Gloria's jaw to drop.

The waitress leaned in, "You wanna lie by the beach, just go out the white gate follow the brick pathway and you can see the water. There's chairs in the sand with umbrellas. Great place to catch a few Z's. It might do you some good." She smiled, her eyes crinkling. When she walked away with the tray Raymond noticed her tidy waist, the swell of her hips, her sure movements.

"Great idea." Raymond reached into his wallet took out some bills and placed them on a plate. "Let's finish these first," he said and Gloria gulped hers down, flicking her tongue over her upper lip, her eyes like scars. He would have to tell her to get rid of that garish pink lipstick. It didn't do her justice. After a while of nothing to say, he pushed their empty glasses aside and headed off with Gloria, who was looking a little dazed.

It was between lunch and rush hour and the lobby was deserted. The wood veneer elevator opened and they stepped inside. Gloria leaned against the wall and tried to speak, "I have to tell you that . . ."

Raymond panicked How long did it take for the pills to set in? He figured about twenty minutes max. She would not be ready for the knockout blow coming at her. When he got to the door, he was huffing and puffing from exertion, from trying to move her along the hallway, dragging her against the wall.

He had the keycard in his hand but was so worn out that he had trouble inserting it into the slot. "Here," she said. "You're holding it upside down." He tried to focus, but the image of the card was blurry. She snatched it away from him and he just made out the green light going on when she moved behind and body-checked him into the room.

"Hey, wait a minute . . ." As he toppled to the floor inside the room, the last clear image he had was of Gloria's face distorted, staring down at him as if inside a fisheye lens.

He came to on a damp carpet, barely able to breathe. The smell was dank, moldy and he felt excruciating pain radiate throughout his left arm. He made out voices as if in a tunnel. He could hear Gloria's unmistakable harsh whine. She had the kind of whisper that carried. He strained to hear the other voice but could not even tell if it were male or female. No shaft of light penetrated his vision before he was overwhelmed by a terrifying spasm of pure physical nausea. He opened his mouth to speak and spittle drooled down his chest.

With horrifying clarity he realized that he was in full-blown cardiac arrest, probably set off by the medication Gloria had given him. He had drank her glass somehow or had she given something else to him? He wanted to believe that she would help him if she only knew how badly off he was but he couldn't speak. She walked into the room and looked at him with kindness, "It'll pass," she said and he tried to answer but he couldn't. He imagined that they would get rid of the pills in the cupboard. In between spasms, he raised his eyes and saw her pull at her hair and chew her lurid pink lips and he wanted to make her stop or she would ruin her face. She stroked the top of his head as he lay trembling. *How would she survive without him?* he thought just before the lights went out.

6. Block

Mike Dennis

I took one look around the room before I walked out. It was like any one of thousands of identical Best Western rooms, except for the sheets and pillows torn to pieces.

And the bloodstains on the wall.

I put the body in the trunk before going back inside to wash up and clean off my hunting knife. Good thing it got dark early this time of year. I'd've hated to have to do it in broad daylight, even though I wrapped her in the hotel bedspread. I could dump her in the woods on old Highway 10 south of town on the way home. This way the animals could have a feast and I could get home in time for dinner.

The bitch shouldn't've said those things to me.

~~~

I noticed the leaves in the driveway as I pulled in, as well as the trashcans still sitting on the curb. What the hell was I paying Dougie his allowance for, anyway? Karen kept saying, "Oh, he's only seven years old. He'll learn." Sure, he'll learn. He'll learn somebody else'd do these chores if he didn't.

The second I opened the door, I was hit with the irresistible aroma of something garlicky cooking in the kitchen. I just loved that smell.

"Honey, I'm home!"

Karen bounced out of the kitchen, wiping her hands on her apron. "Oh, hi, dear. How was your day?" She put her hands to my cheeks, planting a soft kiss on my mouth.

She felt so inviting right here at that very moment. I wanted to lose myself in her. She was so warm, so loving. Not like …

"A day like all days." I smiled back at her. "When you're waiting at the end of it, it's got to be a great day."

She gave me another playful peck and turned back for the kitchen.

"The empty trashcans are still out in front," I said, following her. "And there are leaves all ov – "

She spun around abruptly. Her smile was still there.

"Don't be such a grouch," she said.

"But Dougie hasn't brought the trashca – "

"Oh, Ray." She shushed me with a soft index finger to my lips. "Cut him a little slack. He's only seven years old."

"But he's got to learn – " I tried to speak around her index finger, which was by now pressed harder against my lips.

"Honey, you can't turn him into a worker drone at such a young age."

There was that "worker drone" crack again. I knew what she meant. One of her sly little jabs at me. Just because I worked for a big company and dealt with complex formulas and computers, she thought I was some kind of faceless number buried in the middle of some impersonal corporate roster.

Well, I wasn't.

"Now let me get your dinner ready, okay?"

She turned back to the simmering masterpiece. I headed for the den and the evening paper.

I removed the sheathed knife out of my briefcase and put it away moments before Dougie came scampering into the room.

"Hi, Dad!"

He ran into me with a tight hug. His little head touched my waist.

I ran a hand through his tousled yellow hair. From up here, I couldn't see his face but I could feel his smile. I squatted down and returned the hug.

"How's my little man?"

"Pretty good," he replied through his infectious gap-toothed smile.

"And how was school today? Anything exciting?"

He went on a little about school, but I kept thinking about dinner. The aroma was stronger than ever, and I was getting hungry.

Pretty soon, Dougie sped back to his room and I settled in with my paper. After a minute or two, Karen sneaked into the den.

"Anything in the news?" she said, startling me.

"Listen to this." I folded the paper to the article I just read. "A man was shot and killed last night as he was getting out of his car at a restaurant. Right in front of his wife, no less. For the money in his pocket!" I tapped the paper for emphasis.

Karen let out a gasp. "How horrible! Where did it happen?"

"Up on the North Side. Just across the river."

"Did they get the one who did it?"

"No, but the wife gave them a description. Typical. A couple of street punks trying to impress each other." I tapped the paper again, only this one was more of a backhand slap. "He was an architect. God, he *built* things. And now ..."

Karen shrugged. "That's just awful. His poor wife." Then she added, "You know, honey, I worry a lot about you working downtown like you do. Coming down those elevators into that creepy parking garage. Anything could happen. I just don't know what I'd do if – "

I pulled her to me, throwing my arms around her. It was kind of awkward, me in the recliner, her standing, but we exchanged our affection with each other anyway. As she ran a hand through my hair, I told her there was nothing to worry about.

She moved back into the kitchen, promising dinner in a couple of minutes, while I reflected on what she said. She was right about the building and the parking garage. I wasn't at all comfortable leaving work, but I didn't want to admit it to her. You know, these last three or four years, what with the rising crime downtown, I found myself looking over my shoulder whenever I walked through that garage. I usually had to park a good distance from the elevators and with my heels clicking on the concrete, I felt like a target.

That's the problem, you know. We're all targets for these scumbags who go around terrorizing and killing everybody. They just want to be cool, or they want to prove their manhood, or they want your money, or all three, I don't know ... at any rate, these days no one is safe anymore.

~~~

She put down her pencil. Reaching for her glass of bourbon, she leaned back in her swivel chair and exhaled. She'd gotten this book off to a good start. These were some pretty decent pages.

The idea for the book came from a movie she saw last week in the middle of the night. She forgot the name, but it was a black and white movie from around 1960.

It was about these four couples who lived in the middle-class suburbia of that time. They all sort of looked alike – you know, the men wore suits and skinny ties, and the women wore dresses around the house – but their appearances belied their individual dreams and flaws.

Then she remembered somebody saying, "Things are never as they seem." Suddenly, the idea popped into her head of a *Leave It To Beaver*-type family, where the loving husband and father is a crazed psychopath.

She sipped at her bourbon, then shook a cigarette loose from the dwindling pack and lit it. After that first satisfying drag, she sat back to reread the pages.

The beginning was solid. She felt it dropped the reader right into the story. That was very important, getting the reader into the story, especially for her kind of fiction.

These weren't multi-generational sagas she was writing. She couldn't afford the luxury of two or three chapters of exposing a wide array of characters, carefully setting up a dense plotline that would carry the reader through a hundred years of a family's history and a seven-hundred-page book. No way.

Her books were different. The first couple of sentences, one paragraph at most, were all she had to grab the reader.

She eyed the shelf above her desk. It contained the slim hardcover versions of all nine of her novels. And on the wall above those were the two Edgar Awards she'd received for best mystery novel two years running.

She reflected back on how she'd taken the literary world by storm back then, coming out of nowhere the way she did.

And did she ever! Was it really thirteen years ago?

~~~

Originally a housewife, her husband traded her after ten years for a newer model. Fortunately, there were no children involved, so she packed up and drove to Fort Lauderdale. She'd grown weary of those harsh Michigan winters, and she desperately needed a little warmth in her life for a change.

Well, it wasn't long before she finally sat down to write something. She'd been feeling the urge for some time, so she plopped down at her table with a pencil and blank white paper. She didn't even own a typewriter, much less a computer – they were just starting to get popular back then. So she sat there, looking at that plain white paper for what seemed like forever.

Nothing came.

More forever. More nothing.

Finally, an opening line came to her. She jotted it down, and that led to couple of more lines. A central character developed out of these lines and she kept going. Other characters began to suggest themselves and pretty soon the whole thing resembled a novel in the making. She wrote every waking moment of every day, and three months later, she had the first draft of *Death On Top*.

It was eventually published, earning her first Edgar and enthusiastic reviews. One of them called it "a chilling first-person report from deep inside the criminal mind". It didn't make the best-seller list because that kind of book is never a bestseller, but it sold well. Plus, the fact that a woman wrote this story of the inner thoughts of a male criminal didn't hurt, either. It was also made into a movie, which became a sleeper-hit.

She had more first-person criminal stories in her, but she went third-person for her follow-up book in order to avoid the "same old same old" label. *Tight Squeeze* won her the second Edgar, along with many shining reviews.

With these two searing novels, Lila Rakubian has established herself as one of the premier crime novelists of the last 50 years.

It was optioned by a movie studio, but the movie was never made. Nevertheless, she climbed to dizzying new heights, making the rounds of all the TV talk shows and magazine interviews.

After a while, her name became synonymous with the twisted scoundrels of her writings. She tried to dispel any notions of similarity between her and her characters by explaining quite clearly that this was only fiction, all made up. But she was so articulate and precise, and utterly lacking in any on-screen emotion, that she came off looking and sounding cold and devilish, that perhaps one of these killer brutes actually did reside deep within her.

Working against her too was her unholy appearance. Her eyes, the color of a chilly blue sky, were hard, set close together. A trace of a slant betrayed a long-ago Asian ancestry. Thin brows flared out from the center with a slight upward turn, and her mouth was a narrow slash. In her teens and twenties, this pinched look was exotic and fetching, attracting men of all kinds.

Now, however, at forty-six, and with these violent novels propelling her into American homes, it was scary.

~~~

Andy stood in the doorway of my house, backlit by the bright morning sun. He hollered up the stairs.

"Ray, you ready?"

I leaned over the bannister from the upstairs hallway. "Be right down, Andy," as I headed into the bathroom.

From up in the bathroom, I heard Karen say, "Come on in, Andy. You know how Ray is, he takes his own sweet time. You might as well have a seat."

By the time I got downstairs a couple of minutes later, Andy fidgeted in the living room, nervously checking his watch.

"Hi, Andy. How's it look out there today? You ready to hit 'em?"

"Ray, we tee off in twenty minutes. You know how particular the club is about making our tee-off time."

I took my clubs out of the hall closet, and slung them over my shoulder. "Aw, we got time. The club's only ten or fifteen minutes away."

"Okay, let's get going. We've got to get there." Andy moved toward his idling car out front while I turned to Karen and gave her a sweet kiss.

"Bye bye, honey. Say, where's Dougie?"

"Oh, he went over to Jason's house. I think they're playing video games."

"Video games? I see you didn't make him pick up his room." I looked out at the yard. "And there're leaves all over the lawn again!"

She kissed me again. "Ray, quit being such a slave driver. He's only seven years old. You can't expect him to ..."

Aha! There it was. I knew it. Another little cut where she thought it would hurt. That crack about being a slave driver.

Can't a father instill a little discipline in his own son? Of course, she wouldn't know anything about that, since no one had ever disciplined her at any time in her life. But believe you me, I know a few things that could snap her into line.

And there were times when she certainly needed it.

Then there was Andy. Him and his damn watch. All this stuff about how we've got to get there right on the dot or else. I was really getting tired of it. I'd have done something about it, except that he worked in human resources at our company. Our weekly golf game made us friends, and it was always good to have a friend in that department these days, what with the company's stock dropping like a rock and all the layoffs.

~~~

Lila looked up at the clock. Ten after three. God, where had the time gone? A minute ago, it seemed like it was only midnight.

She crushed out the stub of her cigarette, then drained the bourbon from her rocks glass. Once she set her pencil down on top of the current page, as was her routine, she was finished for the day.

After peeling off her clothes, she reflected on the night's work. About six pages, including the start of chapter five. Laying the groundwork for Ray to kill Andy.

This would be his third murder – his first male victim – and with this one, his unraveling would truly begin. He would slowly lose control of himself, ultimately killing Karen in the process in a grisly, blood-drenched scene. Described, of course, in his own inimitable voice.

She crawled into bed and turned on the classical music station, setting the sleep timer. Come ten in the morning, she would hop out of bed and take a shower. Then, all refreshed, she'd dash down to her office, resuming her writing till she broke for lunch around one-thirty.

Just like always.

~~~

The ringing telephone roused her mercilessly from a deep sleep.

"H'lo." Her voice was a scratchy mumble, but it got no response.

She tried again. "H'lo." A cigarette cough burst out of her into the phone and she heard a click on the other end. After a couple of tries, she finally got the phone back on its hook, but not before she caught a glimpse of her clock.

Ten till seven.

She cursed and threw her head back down onto the bed, burying it beneath her pillow.

At nine-thirty, she woke up. She didn't feel at all rested and was already upset. She hated to be awakened like that, especially for no apparent reason. Some wrong number or a teenage prank. Why couldn't they have dialed someone else's number?

By ten-thirty she was showered and caffeinated. She brought a second cup of coffee, along with a blueberry muffin, into her office, then took her seat in front of the growing pile of pages.

As she sipped her coffee, she contemplated the story's next turn of events. Her first thought was to follow Ray and Andy to the country club, maybe even follow them out onto the golf course, with Andy getting under Ray's skin more and more. She picked up the pencil, intending to head in that direction.

Then she thought, no, that would be redundant. She already showed how Andy can irritate Ray, so maybe she should just pick them up as they're returning from the golf game. Yes, that's it. Just as Ray is getting out of Andy's car back home, she could show how close Ray was to the edge after being subjected to yet another one of Andy's punctuality lectures. That's it!

She started to write.

~~~

She didn't know how long she'd been staring off into space before she realized she hadn't written anything. The clock said it had only been twenty minutes. But still there were no new words on the paper.

With pencil poised, she started again to write the next paragraph. But ... there was nothing. She sipped heartily at the coffee, looking for the jolt that would take her out of the doldrums. She just wasn't awake yet. That was the problem. Another big sip should do it.

She emptied the cup and went to pour another, thinking of what the very next words would be. No words came during this little walk to the kitchen, but by the time she sat back down, she'd have them.

Back at her desk, she fiddled with the pencil, sharpening it and touching its point to the blank space on the paper. She twirled it in her fingers for a few seconds, then inspected the eraser tip.

She gazed out the window at the silence of her back yard. Her hibiscus needed watering. And for that matter, the traveler's palm didn't look too good, either. Come to think of it, it hadn't rained for over a week, and she hadn't watered since beginning this book. She got up and went out back.

She picked up the hose to refresh her thirsty vegetation while her mind went back to the book.

Ray and Andy come back from golfing. Ray is really agitated over Andy's righteousness, but bottles it all up. This leads to Ray's next murder.

What's the problem? Why can't I get this simple little scene down on paper?

The watering continued. After the hibiscus and the traveler's palm, she went on to the rest of her yard. This was about a ten- or fifteen-minute exercise which always mellowed her out, and sometimes it could even help her overcome these little lulls in her writing. This was really all she needed. Just to relax a little.

And no wonder. After that phone call woke her up this morning, her body was thrown off. She needed to unwind, like she was doing now.

Soon she was back at work, awake, refreshed, and ready to bat out this scene. But after another twenty-minute staring match with the blank page, she blinked, then set her pencil down. She needed to go to the post office, anyway. Good time for a break.

After the post office, she thought up a couple of other errands. Soon it was time for lunch.

She treated herself to lunch at one of those little outdoor cafés down on Las Olas. The weather was perfect and the food was excellent, so she lingered, taking in the delight of the day, while smoking an extra couple of cigarettes.

Around three o'clock, she paid her check, then headed home, in a totally upbeat frame of mind. At last.

But when she got back to her desk, the pencil that rested on her pages seemed hostile and snarling. It seemed to dare her to pick it up, warning of severe consequences.

She looked at it for a minute or two, then got up from the desk once and for all. Today was just not her day. Maybe it was something in the stars, or her biorhythms.

But whatever it was, the book would just have to wait till tomorrow.

~~~

In her dream, her limo was approaching the building where the Book Club Awards were being presented. The only difference was the dizzying Oscar-type atmosphere, complete with red carpet, paparazzi, and a gauntlet of adoring fans. As she pulled up, the door was opened for her. She started to step out, but was knocked back inside the limo by a fierce explosion. She spun her head around, but couldn't find its source.

A few seconds later, another explosion. And another.

She threw her arm outward, groping for the ringing telephone.

She couldn't quite speak yet. "Hmnh."

The line was silent. After a couple of seconds, she stirred awake. "Who is this?" she demanded, her voice coated with sandpaper.

The click on the other end told her the conversation was over. The clock glowed six-fifteen. It was still dark out.

She slammed the phone back onto the cradle.

~~~

That next day was no more fruitful. She sat and stared, drank coffee, went for a walk, even watched TV for a couple of hours. At night, she made a few fumbling efforts at writing the scene, but they just didn't work. Nothing she did could bring those characters back to her.

Oh, she'd had a few false starts before where she'd written sixty or seventy pages before realizing that the book was not shaping up. She had simply walked away from those efforts. That's not unusual for a writer, but this book didn't fit that category. She knew this one was for real. This book begged to be finished.

She could feel the characters in her, the way she always could when she was on the right track. They lived in her, they really did. When she was on, she knew her characters as well as she knew herself. Ray Owens was one of her best characters ever, on a par with Barney Sands in *Death On Top*.

No, she couldn't abandon this book. It was there. She just had to drag it out of herself.

But she wasn't going to do it on this day. Or the next. Or the next.

And each morning, at some ungodly hour, the ringing phone would shake her out of her sleep. By now, she was just picking up the phone an inch or two before dropping it back onto the hook in one fluid motion.

Finally, on the sixth day of her drought, the phone rang on schedule and she did the pickup-hangup thing, but then it rang again a few moments later.

Lila grabbed it off the table, shouting into it, "Who the hell is this?"

Her hair was matted over her forehead, partially blocking one of her reddened eyes, while lines creased her face from poor sleep. She sprang up on one elbow at the sound of a voice on the other end.

"I have a collect call for anyone fr – "

"What? Wha – who the hell is this?"

The operator repeated: "I have a collect call for anyone from Ray Owens. Will you accept the charges?"

She froze. Her gaze fell upon the clock, which read six-twenty. She didn't see it. She didn't see the first light of day trickling into her room. She didn't even breathe.

"Will you accept charges on a collect call from Ray Owens?"

"R-Ray ... Ray Owens?"

"Yes. Will you accept the charges?"

She could barely move her lips. "Ray Owens is – is – he doesn't – I mean – "

"Ma'am, I need to know if you will accept these charges."

"N-no ... I ..."

"Did you say no? You will not accept the charges?"

Suddenly a male voice interceded, a calm presence in this churning mess. "She'll take the call, operator. Just tell her again it's from Ray Owens."

Lila's composure crept back into her. She now sat upright, fully awake.

What kind of a gag was this? Who knew?

But that was just it. No one knew about Ray. Absolutely no one.

She never let anyone read her manuscripts until she completed them, and she never discussed names of characters with anyone, not even her agent or editor, until she turned it in. Names were always subject to change. So how did they know about him?

"Who is this?" she demanded.

"The caller says he is Ray Owens. Will you accept the charges?"

"All right, all right," she said. "I'll accept the charges, operator."

"Go ahead, sir."

"Hello, Lila."

"Listen, you. Who are you and how do you know about Ray Owens?"

She reached for her cigarettes.

"Lila, I *am* Ray Owens."

With quivering hands, and with the telephone receiver propped between her cheek and her shoulder, she managed to pull a cigarette out of the pack and get it lit.

"Ray Owens is a *character*, for Chrissake! Now who told you about him?"

"Lila honey, nobody told me about him. I am him. You named me."

She puffed furiously on her cigarette while wracking her brain trying to sort this all out. Whom did she tell about this novel? She couldn't remember anyone.

"What's this all about? What do you want?"

"You know this little problem you've been having recently? About continuing your novel? Well, it's not exactly your average writer's block."

She shook her head. Was all this really happening?

"Get to the point. And tell me who you really are or else I'm hanging up."

"I told you, Lila. This is Ray." His voice was so soothing, she thought, just the way she created Ray-the-character's voice. "And to prove it, I live down in the south suburbs of an unnamed midwestern city at 1410 Pine Grove Terrace."

A chill suddenly swept up her spine, outward over her whole body. She created that address, but hadn't even used it yet. She planned to mention it toward the end, when the police came to take Ray's corpse away.

And she never mentioned it to anyone.

He went on: "And our lawn is usually a mess because *someone* I know won't make someone *else* rake the leaves."

Her eyes widened. The chill still covered her like a light November snow.

"Who ... are ... you ..."

He chuckled, good-natured all the way. "It's Ray, sweetie. It's your boy, Ray."

"You can't be Ray. I told you, he's a character in my book. I made him up."

"Lila, please. I prefer to say you 'gave me life'. I know that's how you feel about me. And about all your characters. That's how you can get so close to us. That, and the fact that you write your books in longhand, rather than on a computer."

Another hit right between the eyes.

That was one of her secret little techniques she developed. He was right. Writing in longhand did indeed get her much closer to her characters. It made her feel as though she was the maternal, life-giving force. Not until she was ready to turn a manuscript over to her agent did she put it onto her computer and print it up.

"How do you know ..." Her voice barely registered into the phone, then trailed off.

He ignored her half-question. "Well, anyway, as I mentioned a minute ago, you're not suffering from standard-issue writer's block."

This is not happening! This is NOT happening!

"What are you getting at?"

She extinguished her cigarette and reached for another.

He said, "We've gone on vacation."

"What? What?"

"I said, we've gone on vacation. I took Karen and Dougie down to Disney World for a few days."

"Disney World?"

"Right. You ever been there? Oh, let me tell you, it's not just for kids, you know. It's really pretty fascinating. Anyway, we spent a few days there, and now we're in Key West, enjoying the sunshine."

"What – what do you mean, you're on vacation?"

"Just what I said. We took off for a while."

"And you're saying that's why I can't – "

"That's why you can't continue the story. Exactly. Because we're not there."

"Well ... well, when are you ... coming back?"

"Ah, that's what I wanted to talk to you about, Lila. We have some important matters to discuss."

"Important matters?"

"Yes. Very important."

"What matters are these?"

"I really can't talk about this over the phone, Lila. Can you come down to Key West? It's not that far from Fort Lauderdale. Just a little under two hundred miles."

Lila now got out of bed and stood up straight.

"Key West? Listen, whoever you are, if you think I'm driving all the way to Key West to meet with someone who says he's a *fictional character*, you're crazy! You hear me? You're out of your mind."

"You know, right now, you probably feel like you're the one who's going out of her mind. But that's okay. Really it is. I know this is unusual." His voice was still calm and level, but he modulated it downward ever so slightly. "I wasn't kidding about this being a matter of the utmost importance. You've got to come."

"I'm not going to Key West and that's that. Now if you want to play your little game, we can do this over the phone, but I'm not – "

"Please come, Lila," he interrupted. He gave her directions to the hotel. Then he added, "We're in room one-sixteen."

"Go to hell," she yelled, and slammed the phone back down, nearly knocking her ashtray off the bedside table.

~~~

The drive to Key West was uncomfortable. Friday afternoon traffic clogged the two-lane thread linking the island chain with the rest of the country. Not only that, she spent a good deal of time following a boat being towed by an SUV. Her car CD player had quit functioning, so she turned to the radio, which could only deliver in-again, out-again stations up and down the Keys. The temperature was warm, although occasional heavy showers spotted the way, most of them coming while she was crawling along behind the boat.

In the two days since the phone call, she tried desperately to continue the book, writing anything that came into her head, anything at all, just to get words on paper. But nothing made sense. In the end, it was only gibberish. The characters and the story just weren't there.

Finally, after several spilled glasses of bourbon and quite a few broken pencils, she stormed out of the house and into her car, heading down the turnpike toward US 1 and the Keys.

One thing was important, though. She had to make certain that no one, absolutely no one, learned of this little incident. Whoever this guy was, whatever he wanted, she'd straighten it out with him, getting his assurance that nobody would find out that she drove two hundred miles to talk with a fictional character.

She could just see it now. Once the word got out, she'd be getting hysterical middle-of-the-night phone calls from people claiming to be Captain Ahab and Don Corleone.

~~~

Key West rose on the horizon to meet her in the late afternoon, and not long after arriving on the island, she saw the hotel, just as he said she would. The rain let up, and the sun made a good try at peeking through the clouds.

Room one-sixteen was around back. She drew up to the door with more than a little anxiety, remembering the scene in *2001: A Space Odyssey* where both the ape-men and the spacemen approached the monolith with exactly the same apprehension.

Moments after her knock, the door opened and there he stood.

Her gasp was barely perceptible, but he caught it. He had the look, all right. Medium height and weight, sort of handsome, but not in a movie-star way. Light brown hair, cut in the style of a corporate company man. Bland blue golf shirt and cuffed khaki pants.

Precisely the way she'd pictured – no, *created* him.

She scanned him further. There was that little boyish twinkle in his eye that endeared him to Karen, the same twinkle that so cleverly concealed the grisly demon that resided behind it. His smile appeared genuine.

She looked around her, around the parking lot, slowly shaking her head, wondering if she was hallucinating all of this, maybe for some other quirky novel. Would she come to any minute now? Would she be back home, picking up her pencil?

"Yes, Lila," he said. "It's really me."

He extended a hand and she shook it limply.

"Please come in." He gently guided her into the room.

A couple of suitcases lay open, showing clothing of a man, woman, and child. Other clothing hung on a rod back by the bathroom. A laptop lay closed and silent on the little round table. There was no one else in the room.

"Karen took Dougie to the aquarium and to a movie. I had to stay here and catch up on some work." He gestured toward the laptop. "It's too bad they couldn't be here. I know they'd love to meet you. You'd enjoy meeting them, too, you know, they've got all the right – "

"My God!" she interrupted. "Good *God!* You – you really *are* him, aren't you?"

He smiled again. "Of course I am, Lila. I've been trying to tell you that."

"But ... but you're fictional! How ... how can you be standing right here? I mean, I made you up!"

"Like I told you on the phone, Lila. I prefer that you say 'gave me life'. It sounds more, shall we say, more human that way."

She couldn't wipe away the disbelief that smeared itself all over her face, but he kept on.

"You just did a great job, so let's leave it at that, okay?"

He led her over to the table with the computer. They each took a chair.

"Now that I think of it, it's probably best that Karen and Dougie aren't here, because I don't really want them to hear what we've got to talk about."

"You don't?"

"No. This is really between you and me."

"Between ... you ... and me?"

He adjusted himself in the chair to face her more directly.

"Yes, but first, Lila, I must have your word that you believe I'm Ray Owens. That you really and truly believe it."

"I don't see how this is happening, but ... but yes. Yes ... I guess I do believe it."

"No, now, there can be no guessing. You must really and truly believe that I'm Ray."

She lowered her head slightly, pressing her thumb and index finger to the center of her eyebrows. Then, much to her own amazement, she heard herself say, "Yes, Ray. I really believe it."

Because by now, how could she not?

"That's wonderful! Now we can continue on a levelheaded, equal basis, like two intelligent adults. Can I get you some water? Or maybe a soft drink? We've got some orange soda in the cooler. And I think maybe some root beer."

"No. No, thank you. Let's just ... get on with it."

"Fine." He leaned forward a little. He was still genial, but the smile had vanished. "Lila, the reason I asked you to come down here today – and I'm very grateful that you took the time to do it – is this: I don't like where the story is going."

"You what?"

"I don't like where you're taking the story. Where you're taking *me*."

"What do you mean, you don't like it?"

"I mean, I know about your plan to have me kill Andy, and then my boss, and then ... then, eventually Karen. And I want to tell you that I don't like it."

"I don't get this."

"Lila, I don't want to kill Andy, and I definitely don't want to kill Karen."

"But you're going to. That's how I've plotted the story."

"Well, you're just going to have to change it, because I'm not going to kill Andy or Karen."

"Ray, you don't understand. That's the strength of the plot. You start off killing a couple of women for various reasons buried deep within your psyche. But then, you gradually become unhinged and start killing people close to you. And because I'm writing it in first person, it's your voice the readers are hearing all the way."

"Yes, *my* voice!" He rapped the table with his knuckles. "And it's *me* who your readers are going to hate! And who could blame them? A man who kills his own wife."

"Ray, take it easy. It's just fiction."

Calm returned to his face and voice. "Lila, you must understand. I love Karen very much. I would never do anything to harm her. She's the mother of my child, for God's sake. How could I hurt her? I love her."

"I told you. Pressure builds up inside you from all these little things that bother you. It builds and builds, and pretty soon you can't take it anymore. And you go ballistic. I've given this plot a lot of thought, believe me. It's going to be a great book."

He sat back in the chair.

"Yes, I'm sure. A great book. And you certainly need one of those, don't you? Let's see, your last three books – or is it four now? – have all been with different publishers, am I right? Each one under a one-book contract, and when it doesn't sell, they drop you. Right again? Face it, Lila. You've been coasting on your reputation for several years now. You need a hit."

She squirmed and said, "Well, my sales haven't been what maybe they should be, but the publishing business is changing. You don't see it because … well … because you don't exist, but the business is changing. The digital rev – "

"Oh, stow it, Lila. You need a hit, plain and simple. You need to restore the shine on your faded reputation. Come on. Admit it."

"All right, I could use a little boost right now. But I'm going to get it with this book. That's what I'm trying to tell you. This will make the difference."

"Yes, except I'm not going to kill Karen. Or Andy, either, for that matter. And that's final."

"Ray, I don't – you don't understand. I … am the writer and you … are the character." She pointed toward him and herself for emphasis. "I decide where the story goes, and you do what I write."

He stood up.

"Well, not this time, Missy! If you think I'm going to murder the woman I love over some little argument or something, you're ver-ry sadly mistaken, you got me? And I suppose I die in the end, making Dougie an orphan? Ha! No way, José!"

Lila shook her head, as if there were cobwebs that needed clearing out. She really wanted a drink right then.

"Ray, I've already decided this. You do these things because it's in your *character*. This is how you are."

"It's *not* how I am, goddammit!" He slammed the table, startling Lila. "I'm not some common murderer. I'm not one of these animals that goes around murdering people willy-nilly, like those street scum criminals!"

"But Ray, you killed those two women in the first three chapters."

"That's not the same thing! They had it coming. They were ... they were ..."

"They were two women who made you very angry. Angry enough to hack them to death."

"But they had it *coming*. Like I just told you. What's the matter, you weren't listening? Not paying attention, as usual? They *had it coming!*"

Tiny droplets of sweat beaded up over his upper lip and on his forehead. A blush of blood reddened his face.

"It's not like these street punks who go around murdering decent hard-working people just to take their money or whatever." He suddenly slapped the table with his palm, but hard. "There! That's it. There's who you should write about. One of those ... those pieces of human garbage. Give *him* life and let him kill *his* wife or whoever. But leave me and Karen *alone*."

"All right, Ray. This conversation is over. I can't talk to you. I'm getting out of here."

She stood up to leave.

He grabbed her by the neck with one hand and flung her onto the bed. His strength surprised her, but then it shouldn't have, because he'd done this before.

He leaped on top of her, knees on her arms and holding her mouth shut with one hand. Frantically, Lila's eyes widened, nearly popping out of her head, as she saw his free hand emerge from under the pillow holding a large hunting knife.

~~~

He took one look around the room before he walked out. It was like any one of thousands of identical Best Western rooms, except for the sheets and pillows torn to pieces.

And the bloodstains on the wall.

7. Murder in the Ivory Tower

Hal Howland

Olivier Jacquard mounted the podium and smiled at the eighty-seven young musicians arrayed before him, comfortable in the knowledge that nearly every one of them hated his guts. It was only the second orchestra rehearsal of the term, but Jacquard's reputation was firmly established throughout the music school and across the campus. Jacquard had earned the permanent enmity of the college maintenance crew during several years when the outdated concert hall was being renovated and the orchestra was forced to perform in various unsuitable spaces throughout the crumbling institution.

Jacquard's philosophy was *Reach them young.* In his career both as a second-rate oboist and as a third-rate conductor, he had met few musicians whose opinions of conductors were not rooted in fear, disrespect, mistrust, unvarnished hatred, or all of these. By acting the part of the fire-breathing despot of cartoon fame, Jacquard was merely preparing his tender charges for the real world.

Typically, Jacquard chose to begin the season's rehearsals with the most difficult and least programmable piece in his ever-growing repertoire of unlistenable modern scores. These works invariably required a large battery of esoteric percussion instruments that no student musician could be expected to possess, which gave Jacquard sufficient opportunity to humiliate the bottom-dwelling drummers for their reliable ignorance. "Ze composer calls here for ze *tambourin de Provençe* to be played *fortissimo* on ze shell with ze *rute du bois,* and you give me a tom-tom tapped with wire brushes?" he seethed at a cute freshman. "Does a violinist arrive without his bow? A clarinetist without his reed?"

The shivering girl was determined not to weep, but her knees would not stop knocking together.

"Go back to ze storage room, and do not return here without ze proper equipage!"

It would not have occurred to Jacquard that neither this nor any other average American college would have owned a *tambourin de Provençe* or the crude fistful of twigs that a German romanticist might have observed slapping the side of a marching bass drum during a village festival. Jacquard saw himself as the modernist equivalent of those self-satisfied historians who spend their careers replicating the music of Haydn and Mozart with the fetishistic conviction that sound quality and intonation must never interfere with authenticity. And Jacquard failed to notice the student's return several minutes later, armed with a disintegrating swing-era field drum whose bottom head was missing, or to appreciate the ingenuity with which the girl had raided a janitor's closet for a whisk broom.

At rehearsal's end, having effectively dashed his young players' hopes of finding anything in the piece that resembled melody, harmony, or natural rhythm, Jacquard smiled to himself and returned the heavily annotated score to his flaking leather satchel. Luxuriating in eighty-seven visual daggers as he stepped down from the podium, the maestro exited the room just as a high-pitched scream emanated from backstage.

Being closest to the alarming sound, the percussionists interrupted the tedious disassembly of their sprawling gear and rushed to the source.

On the floor at the foot of the darkened spiral staircase leading to the lighting booth lay the impeccably dressed and profusely bleeding supine body of the one person in the music school held in lower universal esteem than Jacquard himself: dean Ineke Maarten. Dr. Maarten had apparently been struck or perhaps even shot in the back of the head, and the warped floorboards were angled such that a great deal of blood had pooled under her shoulders and was seeping into one of a dozen Chanel suits Dr. Maarten wore like uniforms. Dark red liquid soaked the pink wool tufts. The immaculate condition of Dr. Maarten's smart new black pumps – the once-pretty administrator's physical attributes remained two sculpted calves that looked incapable of supporting a figure of some considerable bulk – disabused any theory that Dr. Maarten might have fallen down a precarious flight of metal stairs she would never have climbed in a hundred years.

Olivier Jacquard was already enjoying a decadent lunch of fried chicken, buttered garlic mashed potatoes, collards, and espresso in the faculty dining hall up the hill by the time a small contingent of police descended on the music building, strung up yards of yellow tape, and fanned out to interview students, faculty, and staff.

Ineke Maarten's murder was especially unwelcome news to Dr. Angela Fiorello, the assistant dean of music who had hoped she would never face the possibility of taking over the department and who was as popular as Dr. Maarten was not. The still trim, attractive blonde had long ago discredited stereotypes of the massive warrior soprano in a dazzling career that had charmed audiences in every European opera house. Dr. Fiorello enjoyed administrating even less than she had enjoyed teaching, but it was the logical academic trajectory. Effervescent in small gatherings, she had a mortal fear of public speaking and a healthy distaste for fund-raising, two chores that now would dominate her schedule. She hoped the emotional cost of these despised activities would not erode the joy she had derived from the company of students and the less neurotic members of the faculty.

The police would find no shortage of institutional suspects in the case of Dr. Maarten's demise. In addition to her image as a caustic, high-strung bitch who would have sold her mother's wedding ring for a photo opportunity with some potential donor, Dr. Maarten presided over a hornet's nest of dysfunctional geniuses whose daily lives were a litany of numbing repetition and unrealized potential. Aside from a few legitimate virtuosi whose commitment to the arts compelled them to pass on to future generations what they had learned in their distinguished if unaffordable performing careers, the faculty contained more than a few mediocre pedants who had collected their undergraduate *and* graduate degrees from this same institution and simply had hung around long enough to have been offered an office as a means of clearing the hallways. These hacks taught private lessons on their chosen instruments and moderated annual seminars on a variety of minor topics, recycling the notes they had taken not so many years before as students, ensuring a perpetual supply of overwritten dissertations on subjects as riveting as an examination of the atypical viola part in the second movement of some forgotten string quartet. One could hear in these individuals' conversation the years of boiling resentment aimed at a dystopian machine that had stripped away their brilliance and reduced them to ivy-crowned ridicule. Those in this population who led credit-earning ensembles behaved like petulant teenagers whenever the school production manager was obliged to point out the technical impossibility of realizing their aesthetic delusions. Witnessing their twitchy demeanor before and during a performance applied a refreshing comic balm to an otherwise excruciating musical experience. The semifamous director of the wind ensemble actually referred to his unseasoned players as "my people," as though they too were a force to be reckoned with.

The U-shaped, two-story music building, including a dank basement filled with priceless instruments, had begun its existence in the nineteenth century as a convent, complete with Inquisition decor. This design proved ideal for a conservatory: dormitory cells became practice rooms and offices, offices became classrooms, the dining room was transformed into an ample but acoustically infuriating rehearsal hall, the mother superior's quarters provided adequate space for a respectable music library, and the chapel remained just that, a necessary refuge.

Many of the pupils earned pocket money with work-study jobs on the stage crew, in offices, or as teachers' aides and therefore could be found in various semiprofessional capacities throughout the school. But on their own the students ganged together in the cliques of their concentrations and rarely commingled: the fruity voice majors and music-theater extroverts hung out upstairs, not far from the austere organ majors whose extra pairs of shiny shoes were seen more often dangling from their backpacks than dancing across the maple pedal board; downstairs roamed the jive-talking hipsters whose membership in the jazz ensemble distinguished them from the mere mortals who made up the bulk of the instrumental program and whose inability to improvise pointed them straight down the path of self-perpetuating academic failure; the loud brass jocks' goofy behavior had many a string and woodwind player fantasizing about life beyond the proscribed universe of inside harmonies, upbeats, and brief, terrorizing solos; similarly, the guitar majors and piano majors consorted mostly with their own kind, the former identified by their instrument cases, the latter by their stacks of books with bent pages. These kids had emerged from doting families whose own fantasies prevented their ever warning the little darlings that they had entered a field in which most of them stood practically no chance of making a living. Full of themselves as only college students can be, the poor fools trudged on, repeating their futile scales and arpeggios in euphoric denial while the law and engineering majors up the hill were already playing the stock market. The unreality of their pursuit notwithstanding, however, any one of the music students might have greeted the news of Dr. Maarten's death with something other than sadness.

The first day of autumn announced itself with uncharacteristic certainty: a morning that might simply have represented a colorful and slightly cooler version of summer began with a crunchy layer of frost on the grass. People left their homes, saw their breath in the air, and felt cheated.

Cynthia Gérard, a pretty, fortyish brunette professor of piano whose full schedule of private students spared her from classroom teaching, walked toward the music building a bit too close to Dorian Fielding, the pretty, fortyish brunet music librarian – not in any hope of converting the presumably gay scholar, but simply for warmth. "Have you ever noticed that culture and good weather are mutually exclusive?" she asked her colleague.

Dorian had never given the issue much thought, though he was looking forward to his annual winter holiday in Key West. "Hmm. How do you mean?"

"Well," Cynthia continued, "think of the great cultural centers in Europe, and even here: every one of them has seasons, and at least one of those seasons is unbearable. Maybe all art is born of suffering after all. Name a single city that has both nice weather year-round and a decent orchestra, or a serious museum."

Dorian smirked. "Ah. How about Florence? Or Tel Aviv?" His eyes, stinging in the uncustomarily cold air, scanned an imaginary globe. "Madrid? Miami – but their orchestra went broke years ago. Los Angeles!"

"All those places get cold at least part of the year," Cynthia persisted.

"Yeah," Dorian replied. "I guess you're right."

"Let's have lunch sometime this week," Cynthia said. "I want to pick your brain about Key West. Surely a piano teacher can make a go of it in a town that size. This place is really starting to creep me out."

Dorian looked at her with the familiar grimace that had crossed just about everyone's face in the weeks following Ineke Maarten's unsolved murder. "Sure," he said. "How about today?"

"Can't today," Cynthia replied. "My student Becky Gleischmann is giving her first recital of the term, and I told her

I'd hold her hand right up to the downbeat. She's a nervous wreck."

When they reached the door of the music building, Dorian bent down and kissed Cynthia lightly on the cheek. The dry outdoor air produced a static-electric shock that caused both of them to jump.

"Ow!" he said, rubbing his lips.

"*Ow* is right!" she laughed. "Counting the days! Later, dude."

Dorian turned right toward the library, and Cynthia descended the moldy stairs to her studio. Her first task was to flip on the dehumidifier beneath her two nested grand pianos.

Rebecca Gleischmann's recital would begin without promise. Even though her good grades and cheerful personality had endeared her to the faculty, Becky sometimes failed to take to heart the etiquette of classical music. The blonde beauty had been advised to dress appropriately for her term debut, preferably in all black. The midday performance was considered less formal than an evening affair, but Cynthia Gérard had warned Becky not to walk out there looking like Tori Amos.

Cynthia's heart sank when Becky arrived at the studio door wearing a low-cut, midriff-baring sweater and hip-hugging jeans that indeed would reveal too much information when the shapely sophomore sat down at the keyboard. At least both garments were black. And the terrified look on the girl's face led Cynthia to give Becky the benefit of the doubt. She hugged her student, told her she would be great, and put her through her warm-up exercises.

The generalized hiss of faculty disapproval that greeted Becky when she strutted onstage was countered somewhat by her peers' lascivious whispers. The unspoken consensus was that she had better play flawlessly and then offer an apology to Dean Fiorello for her racy attire.

Becky bowed, not too deeply, and took her place at the long black Steinway. Tradition aside, one could not deny the girl's splendid presence.

Becky kept her cool when a freshman's cell phone began ringing during the opening Schubert sonata: that rude occurrence was common enough during concerts by visiting celebrities. (Violinist Itzhak Perlman had delayed a recent performance of the Mendelssohn concerto not only to admonish a listener whose phone had begun playing a Bach two-part invention just before the introduction but also to point out the incorrect composer, genre, and key.) But disaster struck during Debussy's gorgeous prelude *La cathédrale engloutie,* when Becky nailed the thunderous low C and broke the string – an occurrence most pianists live their entire lives without having to experience. The cataclysm that is a snapped low C on a nine-foot concert grand, the present performer's horrified reaction, and the mostly young audience's involuntary laughter brought Rebecca Gleischmann's first recital of the term to a sudden and undignified close. The girl burst into tears, leapt from the instrument, and ran (beautifully) off the stage.

Cynthia rose from her seat, scanned the audience with revulsion, and went up to console her student. As she held Becky in her arms and reminded her never to let a roomful of idiots ruin a performance, Cynthia glanced at her watch and wondered whether she might be able to save lunch with Dorian after all.

The pin-cushion effigy of Ineke Maarten that the cops found hanging in Becky Gleischmann's dorm room turned out to be just one of a number of such treatments discovered throughout the campus, proved nothing, and in fact went some distance toward restoring the impertinent girl's credibility following her aborted recital. That event was rescheduled, Becky showed up in a stunning floor-length black gown and turned in a magnificent performance, and the school's full-time piano technician was given six months in which to overhaul a fleet of neglected Steinways.

Lunch with Dorian Fielding had sent Cynthia Gérard straight to her computer to begin plotting her escape to Key West. Continued darkness, cold, pavement, pollution, and perpetual gridlock were no match for the prospect of gliding through the tropical breeze in minimal clothing twelve months a year. She could handle the beautiful three-hour oversea drive from Key West to Miami for the occasional cultural fix that a town of twenty-five thousand dropouts could not be expected to provide. Cynthia would wait until near the end of the semester to submit her resignation. But when she told Becky Gleischmann confidentially of her plans, the mischievous blonde surprised her teacher with a thorough knowledge of the Southernmost City's comprehensive menu of lesbian and bisexual recreation.

"I'll e-mail you some links," Becky smiled. "Let me know if you ever need to see a familiar face." The women embraced, and Becky paused at the door to confirm that her blushing mentor had got the message.

Olivier Jacquard acceded to the new dean's polite request to offer an audience-friendly program for the fall orchestra concert. He reluctantly tabled the cacophonous epic with which he had opened the semester and presented a well-balanced compromise consisting of Beethoven's Third *Leonore* Overture, Mozart's Piano Concerto no. 21, featuring the celebrated Rebecca

Gleischmann, and, after some administrative arm-twisting and several marathon rehearsals, Bartók's *Music for Strings, Percussion, and Celesta*. (Jacquard's case for the once-daunting Bartók included the work's prominent role in the hit films *Being John Malkovich* and *The Shining*.) Becky was in the dressing room changing back into street clothes when Jacquard pointed to the adorable Korean freshman timpanist Seung-Eun Lee for a solo bow that only briefly would have dampened Becky's moment in the sun.

Weeks became months. As inescapable snow filled gutters, melted and refroze on worn campus paths, and became sooty gray slush at splashing crosswalks, the police were no closer to discovering Ineke Maarten's killer.

The former dean of music had been a lifelong opera buff, and the school's international reputation rested almost solely on its lavish devotion to that expensive genre. Much of Dr. Maarten's ceaseless fund-raising was a by-product of an obsession that nearly had bankrupted the institution on more than one occasion. The season before the dean's murder had marked one hundred years since the nuns had vacated the premises, and to recognize that milestone Dr. Maarten had mounted a chilling production of Poulenc's *Les Dialogues des Carmélites*. The city newspaper had praised "world-class" performances by several student singers and an "unforgettable" depiction of the final guillotine scene. The offstage device the production office had rigged up to produce the sound effect of the heavy blade severing the praying women's heads was simple enough – a long steel pipe held at a forty-five-degree angle as an oiled gym weight slid down the pipe to a wooden block bolted to a resonating chamber – but it had sent the audience home with visions that indeed would haunt their dreams. The dean of the athletic department, jealous of Dr. Maarten's fiscal acumen, had refused to loan the pampered music school any of his equipment; so the gym weight used for that scene was the sole contribution of the conspicuously fit music librarian, Dorian Fielding.

Some weeks before, after sleepless hours trying to remember some minor detail without which the opera surely would have been a dismal failure, Ineke Maarten had dragged herself from bed and driven to the school at one o'clock on a Sunday morning. For all its gaps and eccentricities, the school boasted one of the best music libraries in the eastern United States; the answer to Dr. Maarten's query was certain to be found on its shelves.

When the dean put her key in the lock and entered the darkened library, she had the vague impression that she was not alone. She could have confirmed this impression without embarrassment by allowing her eyes to adjust to the filtered moonlight and backing out the way she had come in. Instead she switched on the lights – and was astonished to discover Dorian Fielding, math professor Efrem Kuntzler, and freshman piano major Rebecca Gleischmann, all naked, intertwined on the floor near an audio-visual console stacked with pornographic videos. Rarely at a loss for words, the dean merely excused herself, saying, "Dorian, we need to talk," and beat a hasty retreat to the neighborhood bar.

At the emergency meeting in her office the following Monday morning, the dean and the guilty trio had agreed that the incident would remain their secret so long as nothing of the sort ever again took place on school grounds. Fears of a scandal persuaded Dr. Maarten not to fire Dorian, expel Becky, or out Dr. Kuntzler. Having been somewhat adventurous herself as an undergraduate, the dean managed a discreet smirk as the three nervous participants shuffled back out to the courtyard.

But Dorian could not shake the humiliation of being discovered by his boss in such a state, involved not only with an eighteen-year-old student but also with a respected, widely published, married mathematician. He and Becky promised to keep the blunder to themselves, but Dr. Kuntzler did not trust the dean to behave likewise: Dr. Maarten had distinguished herself at more than one cocktail party by broadcasting intimate faculty details that her listeners could easily have done without. Every time Dorian and the dean passed each other in the halls following that unfortunate night, the forced professionalism and the administrator's knowing chuckle reverberated in the librarian's head like a jury's echoing verdict. Dr. Maarten was easy enough to dislike on a good day, but now Dorian could barely stand the sight of her.

Dorian Fielding's eclectic tastes in music ran the gamut from Gregorian chant to the most radical experiments of the avant-garde. He was among a handful of people on campus who appreciated Olivier Jacquard's self-imposed mandate to expose his students to contemporary works they might never hear anywhere else. When Dorian learned that Jacquard was considering the world premiere of local composer Yuri Ulyanovsky's outrageous tone poem *The Martyrs of Tiananmen Square,* which called for not one but three anvils to be struck simultaneously with ball-peen hammers, Dorian realized he had found the solution to his problem.

Dorian approached Jacquard one morning, expressed his fascination with Ulyanovsky's score, and asked permission to make a study copy of it for the library. He promised not to circulate it, and the conductor agreed not to mention the transaction to the somewhat paranoid composer. (Ulyanovsky was wont to stamp his copyright notice on every page of his creations, as though the average listener might find any sanitary use for them.) Score in hand, Dorian attended the first of two rehearsals at which Jacquard would subject his defenseless orchestra to *The Martyrs* and made careful note of the anvils' ear-splitting entrances. On the day of the second rehearsal, he called Dr. Maarten on his cell phone and asked her to meet him backstage for a private chat to ameliorate the uncomfortable atmosphere that had developed between them.

One morning early in March, Cynthia Gérard was finishing her workout at the Island Gym in Key West. The glowing pianist was looking forward to a peaceful walk along Higgs Beach before the first of several afternoon students would arrive at her rented William Street cottage. She had just tossed her towel into the tote bag and was turning toward the door when Dorian Fielding walked in, grinning.

"Well!" she exclaimed. Soaked in sweat, Cynthia shrank slightly from Dorian's easy embrace.

"*Well,* yourself!" he smiled. "Your landlord said I'd find you here. Guess who just moved to town! You are looking at the new music librarian at world-renowned Florida Keys Community College. Brunch?"

Cynthia laughed. "Like this?"

Dorian thought his colleague looked smashing in her tight black leotard, but he did not want to misstep; they had not spoken in months. He just stood there, beaming.

Cynthia reached into the bag for her gray running shorts. "At least let me put these on," she said, blushing.

"I hear Camille's has amazing waffles," the archivist suggested. As the two left the gym, Dorian glanced over at the racks of free weights and smiled to himself.

Once they were seated and their coffee was served, Dorian looked at his watch and said, "I have another surprise for you."

In the next moment, Becky Gleischmann strutted in the door wearing a minuscule red tank top, the smallest white shorts either of them had ever seen, and sea-green flip-flops. She came to the table and placed a hand on Cynthia's shoulder. "Spring break!" she laughed.

8. Loose Cannons

Tom Corcoran

Neither crewman would admit to shooting through the hull, and they weren't ratting on each other. They saw that small hole, two inches aft of a starboard main cabin bookshelf, as the boat's problem, not theirs. I would figure out soon enough which one pulled the trigger. As acting captain, on a choppy port tack across the Stream between Florida and the Bahamas, I regarded the shrugs and moping and damage as expensive bad manners punishable by swimming.

One or both of them had a weapon.

I had two.

~~~

When all this goodwill began, back in the Keys, I almost blew my first clue. It was dusk in Schooner Wharf and the only things winking at me were weather-bleached neon signs. Wilson Gaylord announced his arrival by dropping a two-pound loop of keys on the bar. As if the sheer count of locked vehicles and doors that awaited his whims validated his power and authority. He gave a thumb's-up to Trish Garcia, the bartender. Trish grabbed a rocks glass and turned to reach for the Johnnie Walker Black.

Gaylord nudged my arm. "Brady Dolan. Just the man I was looking for."

"Wonderful," I said. "I was hoping for a cute dinner date."

"Right," he said. "You up for a run? I need my Hunter 39 in Bimini ten days from now."

"Thirty-nine's a fairly new boat," I said. "I've never seen yours."

"It's an oh-nine, the first year for that model. It's the *Swizzle Stick III*, docked at Oceanside."

My reputation is a hassle magnet. I can't bitch about the pay scale, but boat deliveries are nightmares. No matter how much you dig, you have no assurance of a yacht's condition, no clues to hidden problems. There is requisite paperwork – the verification of ownership and notarized travel-permission documents. There will be crew compatibility issues and weather surprises. And, finally, owners have been known to sabotage their boats to collect insurance. I earn every penny.

Bimini, the nearest Bahamian port, made it worse. Boats that stay in Florida, no big deal. Transits to other states aren't too complicated. But sail to another country and you add immigration, customs and that potential search for contraband – drugs, bundles of cash, or tech items prohibited for export.

The most significant fact in this case was that Gaylord had a ten-year reputation for screwing delivery captains out of their pay. Finding damage to the boat, holding back promised cash, writing rubber checks. Mister Buddy-Buddy until time came to square up. There was always a problem.

My problem was the lack of heft in my wallet and bank account.

"What are we talking here?" I said. "Cash, check, smoke, mirrors?"

"I'm talking three-K in gently used hundreds."

Cash is great, I thought, but the amount was too short. Find two crewmen, pay three hundred each, and fly us all back home. Even if I did it with only one helper, three grand didn't cover me for my trouble.

"Crew and provisions?" I said.

"I'll cover wages and airfare," said Gaylord. "The three grand is just for you, and the fuel and fresh water tanks are full. I wasn't thinking food, but I'll boost it by two-fifty."

Those numbers put me closer to the generous realm that I loved so much.

"Tools and repair kits aboard?" I said.

"Three boxes of gear that I've accumulated for years, plus replacement hoses, hose clamps, pumps and gaskets. A set of spare fuses, a cabinet full of operating manuals, a huge first-aid kit and dock line up the ying-yang."

"Any of your personal belongings going into the Bahamas?"

"The boat's clean as a whistle."

All the right answers. I could already feel that wad of cash in my pocket.

"What's my budget for hiring crew?"

Gaylord tossed back the dregs of his drink. "Like I said, don't worry about that. I'll pay them myself. You'll like these guys."

"These guys?"

"They've worked around the boat for me. I mean, at different times, not together, but each one knows the equipment."

I felt a void in the pocket instead of that wad of future dollars.

"I don't sail when I can't pick my own people," I said. "Thanks but no thanks."

"Bear with me," said Gaylord. He raised one index finger and used the other to cue his cell. When the phone lighted he said, "Call Moss."

The phone proceeded to do so.

Not many people with that name, I thought. A call to Moss Hovatter was a good sign. I knew I could work well with the man. Let's see where this goes...

Gaylord lifted the phone to his ear when Moss took the call. "You free to run down to Schooner's right now?" he said. "Ten minutes of your time."

He hung up without receiving an answer.

"Did you hear me say that I prefer to pick my own crew?"

Gaylord waved at Trish, pointed to my beer and his glass requesting fresh ones. "Four grand change your mind?"

Maybe, I thought. But the sudden jump in pay came too easily. That plus some fine advice from a good friend later that night raised the red flag.

"You'll shop for your own groceries, of course," said Gaylord.

"Of course," I said. "I'm picky about my granola bars."

Wilson went through the drill again. He barked at his phone, ordered it to call Oscar – a name I didn't recognize – and asked the man to visit the bar. After he shut down the conversation, he said, "Oscar's been in town a year or so."

~~~

Twenty minutes later, still sitting on the same barstool, nursing the same beer, I had shaken hands with Moss Hovatter and Oscar Raney.

Hovatter looked nautical. All the yachting stores these days and clothing outlets, it doesn't take eighty-five bucks, non-skid shoes and a string on your sunglasses to look nautical. Even sanitation workers look nautical in the Keys. But Hovatter also knew how to sail. He had crewed on boats between Newport and Bermuda in the late nineties. Done a few other things in later years, too, for a lot more than five hundred a day. I assumed he'd decided to lay low for a while, earn some legitimate bucks.

Oscar looked strong, which helps at sea. Clothing old, basic, but clean. Movie star good looks, but a touch of dullness in his eyes. But, what the hell? We weren't hiring computer programmers. The best crew members are five-eight to five-ten. Big enough for serious strength, compact enough for endurance. They're also the most dangerous enemies. You can tell by their facial muscles how much time in their lives they've spent smiling – versus frowning or worrying. Oscar wasn't a smiler.

Wilson Gaylord sent away his prospective sail crew.

I said, "Can I let you know in the morning?"

"My guys will be ready to go bright and early, thirty-six hours from now."

"You said ten days."

"That's the boat," he said. "The boys need to be back SAP."

"You and I have paperwork to do. With a witness present."

"Going formal on me, Dolan?"

"Just making ready the way I always do things."

Gaylord waved his hand as if shooing bugs. "Have it your way. Call me when you have stuff ready to sign. I'll meet you wherever."

"I'll need you to hand me an envelope full of cash before I cast off dock lines."

Gaylord nodded once, dropped two twenties on the bar, snatched his massive key ring and left.

I had spent half my life digging my ass out of garbage generated by my own greed. Once again I had let cash cloud my judgment regarding the shit-to-riches ratio.

~~~

"Hey, baby," said Trish Garcia.

I turned to regard Lou Combs dropping onto Gaylord's still-warm barstool. As a straight-shooting guide and boat broker, Combs had been around the docks for a long time. I had known him most of those years.

"Top of the evening," he said. "How's my true love and her best customer?"

Trish kissed her fingertips and tapped them on Lou's forehead.

"Wilson Gaylord just offered me a delivery gig," I said. "Here to Bimini."

"Paying well?"

"Extremely well, and he's providing crew that I don't have to pay."

"His guys?"

"His guys, and I gave him a tentative 'okay.'"

"Most captains would run away fast. Has he already identified his crewmen?"

"Trotted out two salty dogs. I met each of them twenty minutes ago. One was Moss Hovatter."

"Clockwork, perfect. Can I buy you a beer?"

"Lou, you never buy beer."

"We should talk."

Thank goodness, we did.

~~~

By eight the next morning I was into my usual checklist. I did a GPS plan of the trip with best- and worst-case transits, point to point. People say that modern navigational tools take most of the work out of distance boating, but it's not true aboard sailboats. Much of the work is adjusting to conditions. Sea conditions, wind direction, incoming weather, and calm winds that require judgment regarding the noise of an engine and available fuel supply. Following seas are not the blessing that well-wishers imagine. It's a pain in the ass when open-ocean waves constantly push you off course. Autopilot is for imaginary use only; too often it breaks down in use. Basically, someone has to navigate and steer the boat around the clock.

I also had to figure out why Wilson Gaylord had so readily upped the delivery fee. The yacht would arrive intact – that's how I did business. What else did he want to accomplish? Our meeting to sign the boat transit papers told me nothing. We met in a friend's real estate office, and I gave the duty salesperson a modest restaurant gift certificate for notarizing our autographs. Gaylord smiled a bit, gave me our grocery allowance and a key to his yacht but said little. That meant zilch for insight, more darkness for my worries.

~~~

I reached the dock at Oceanside twenty minutes after sunup the next morning and used my phone camera to document the boat's exterior condition. I surveyed the stubby cockpit, too small for a tall man to grab a topside nap. The innovative dual helm stations suggested twice as much equipment to maintain or to fail at sea. I unlocked the cabin hatch, went below to conduct an interior inspection, and heard an automatic bilge pump kick to life, its outboard splash a comfort. It shut down after only fifteen seconds, an equally reassuring sound that spoke of minimal through-hull leakage. I chucked my nylon backpack onto the aft captain's bunk. It carried two extra LED flashlights, a distress flag, socks, T-shirts, granola bars, tuna in foil packs and a referee's whistle on a lanyard that I hung around my neck, tucked inside my overshirt. I checked for chill in the icebox, turned on the UHF and HF radios at the nav station and started the generator.

Routine checks. None of all that was my real worry on this trip.

When I went topside to activate the GPS and start the boat's motor, I found Moss Hovatter and Oscar Raney on the concrete dock, sipping coffee from Quik Mart cups, scratching their nuts, staring at other yachts. Hovatter looked rested and fresh. Oscar looked like he had spent most of his trip wages right up until dawn. Again using my phone camera, I captured the data pages of each man's passport. Then, with a few gestures and suggestions, I boosted my talented crew into action.

While they trash-canned their coffee cups, stowed their duffels, and removed the sail covers, I emailed my photos to myself and to Lou Combs. The southerly wind direction made it simple to hoist and drop the boat's sails at the dock – an assurance of snag-free cruising. Right on time the cab driver I had paid to shop for us arrived with $150 worth of groceries.

Wilson Gaylord strode down the dock with an envelope at precisely the moment I felt ready to get underway. He nodded to Moss Hovatter, ignored Raney and tossed dock lines as I backed out of the slip. He looked mildly surprised when I pocketed the money without counting it.

~~~

We were fifty yards beyond the channel dogleg south of Oceanside, about to hoist sails, when Lou Combs's flats-fishing skiff, *Tookawile,* passed us quickly on plane. Lou recognized me, slowed abruptly, then swung around to match our speed and direction. His girlfriend, Trish Garcia, the bartender, stood next to him at the console. She used a point-and-shoot to snap pictures of *Swizzle Stick III* and the three of us on deck as the skiff approached our port quarter, nudged up alongside us.

"Ahoy, Dolan," called Lou. "What a boat! Day sailing or going somewhere?"

"Bimini-bound," I said. "A quick delivery. See you in a few days."

"You got a way to cook these, right?" He hoisted a beautiful yellowtail snapper. "We got three and a leftover bag of ice if you want it. We're going in from here, and we decided to have lunch at the Hogfish."

I asked Oscar to stow the ice and handed the fish to Moss so he could clean and prep them for later. While their backs were turned I slipped the four thousand from Wilson Gaylord's envelope to Lou, and he slipped me a thick wad of twenties.

Trish made sure the crewmen were out of earshot, then said, "Gaylord has been sneaking around with Oscar's live-in girlfriend. He's been a billy goat in heat, even though she's a fluff of cotton candy."

"The missing piece to the puzzle," I said. "That explains why he wanted Oscar on this trip. And why he didn't acknowledge him this morning."

"Guilty, guilty," said Trish.

"She's a dandy," said Lou. "Her eyes are pools of blue, but her brain is a shallow puddle."

"Not that Gaylord would know the difference," said Trish.

"Say what?" said Oscar Raney.

I hadn't seen him come back out of the cabin.

Not sure how much he had heard, I said, "Gaylord wanted you and Moss on this transit. He must have more confidence in you than he does in me, but I'm okay with it. We'll get the job done."

"He always treated me right," said Oscar.

"Wish we could join you," said Lou, "but I've got a charter tomorrow."

"I'm worn out on Bimini," said Trish. "I'd probably try to talk you into sailing across to my dream beach in Portugal."

Oscar Raney sidled closer to our conversation. "Pretty lady," he said to Trish, "please don't put that picture of me on Facebook. Half my so-called friends, they learn I'm out of town, they'll break in and relieve me of my television and beer supply."

Trish regarded Oscar's godawful, category five hangover. "Good thing you asked me, sailor," she said. "I'm a Facebook fool. Can I do it when you get back?"

"Whatever."

~~~

I told Moss and Oscar that I wanted to run southeast to pick up the Stream. The winds were due to shift from south to southeast. If a counter-current was running down Hawk Channel, I didn't want to push water all the way to Fowey Rocks.

The plan worked perfectly. We passed Eastern Sambo then, a few miles south of Maryland Shoal, we swung around to 045 to parallel the Keys. With the wind shift and water flow adding several knots to our true speed, we settled on a beam reach, not too flat, not too close-hauled.

We also settled into predictable routine, the chatter of camaraderie. I suggested that we cook the fish for tomorrow's breakfast. Moss floated the idea of a side trip to Paradise Island, across from Nassau. He joked that we could dye our hair silver if we wanted to score with the women in the casino.

Oscar wasn't laughing. He looked like he needed ten hours' sleep. I told him to get some rest because I would need him later. He went below while Hovatter stayed in the cockpit with me, checked the sail settings and showed me where the foul weather gear and safety harnesses were stored.

~~~

Two hours later Oscar appeared at the cabin door, and I asked him to take the helm for a while – to make sure he could deal with a fluky wind and steer a straight course. Hovatter went behind us, took a piss off the stern, then sat in the low side helm station, began to fiddle with the CD player controls. I could have predicted the first squabble almost to the minute. An Earl Klugh jazz selection matched the mid-day relaxation aboard the boat.

"Music imitates chicken scratches and seagulls," said Oscar.

"What's better for you?" said Moss. "Red Solo Cup Time Somewhere Over the Fucking Rainbow?"

Oscar shook his head. "I could use some old Jimmy Reed."

"Rings a bell," said Moss, staring at the horizon, not looking at Raney. "You left one of his CDs on the boat last month. Boss chucked it into the salt water. Skipped the fucker like a flat rock."

Raney, long-faced: "I wondered..."

I settled the topic: "It's too choppy for a CD player right now, anyway. We'll listen to some easy sailing stuff after dark."

They kept up their banter, argued whether it was stupid or smart to play the lottery. They whined about TV shows and Firestone tires. Which of the cheap beers gave you more gas than buzz. Whether they would give their left gonad to get it on with Scarlett Johansson or Bar Rafaeli.

During a brief lull, Oscar looked up at the sky. He pretended to focus on a distant cloud, but I knew he was still too hung over to see clearly.

"You ever imagine how far it all goes?" he said. "How fast it's expanding, and how alone we might be in the universe?"

"You'll be alone the rest of your life," said Hovatter. "It's got nothing to do with expansion, though. You can stop worrying about that. It's because you're an asshole who gets into conversations and won't let anyone else talk even for a minute, or be right about any damned thing."

"How is it you know that?"

Hovatter tapped a winch handle against his palm. Not a cheesy pot-metal handle but a serious Barient still under warranty. Ill will was bubbling up to the surface. I was beginning to figure out the trip's true dynamics.

It occurred to me that Wilson Gaylord might want Oscar Raney farther out of the picture than a three-day voyage. Could he have paid Hovatter to kill Oscar? Maybe push him off the boat after dark?

"After sunset," I said, "I want one of you always down below to monitor Channel 16. Unless we hit a whale, I don't want to see both of you up here until sunrise."

"Monitor the radio?" said Hovatter.

I nodded. "You can take turns sleeping and staying awake to listen. The two times I've almost died in the Gulf Stream, I was saved by a call from the freighter that was about to mow us over. Their radar works better than our eyes. It's a bitch to get T-boned by an oil tanker."

Oscar went first. "Oh, I remember one time..."

I interrupted, showed him the flat of my hand. "One sure thing about sailboat rides, Oscar. It takes a hell of a chat topic to beat the option of silence."

"Does that mean...?"

"Right."

Oscar got the message and shut his trap. Moss Hovatter remained quiet, and I wondered if his mind was filled with noise. I had made it only slightly more difficult for him to push Oscar over the side.

~~~

An hour before daybreak the bullet went through the hull. I was at the helm, half-dozing, when I heard the shot. To this day I don't know why I stayed topside to wait for whatever happened next. What could I learn from a single gunshot? I recall hoping there wouldn't be a second shot, and I knew there were three possibilities. Moss was dead, Oscar was dead or no one was dead. I also considered the chance that the shooter might kill me next. I had to assume that each of us had brought a gun on the trip.

I unsnapped the holster at the small of my back. I waited while the boat pitched down a wave slope and chugged up another.

Hovatter was first to show his face in the cabin hatchway.

"What the fuck?" I said.

His shrug was that of a bad actor trying to portray an Italian waiter.

"Oscar?" I called out.

"Down here monitoring," said Raney. "No freighters calling."

"Why are we playing target practice?"

No response.

"Okay, you won't tell me who took the shot. Tell me where the bullet went."

"Starboard side, mid-ships," said Hovatter. "Two feet above the waterline."

"How will I explain that hole to Wilson Gaylord? You boys going to split the tab to pay for repairs?"

Shrug.

"Okay, Oscar, come on up here. Let me talk to you face-to-face."

Hovatter stepped into the cockpit to make room for Raney. In the dim light from below I saw that neither held a weapon. I stood as well as I could, pretended my footing was secure, then rested my 9mm Beretta Nano against the steering wheel.

"This won't kill you, but it will screw your health insurance forever, so hear me carefully. Both of you, take off your clothes. Oscar, port side. Hovatter, starboard. Take off everything. I want wagging weenies, or you can fucking well swim to the beach."

"Some kind of perv, Captain Dolan?" said Moss Hovatter.

"He wants your butt, not mine," said Oscar.

"Right now shut up or dive in," I said. "I will absolutely shoot you dead. I don't give a shit. Who wants to test me first?"

While they disrobed, I played a few scenarios in my mind. Wilson Gaylord paid Moss to shove Oscar over the side, or shoot him if necessary. Or... he paid Oscar to shoot Moss so that Oscar would be arrested for murder. Maybe Gaylord had told Oscar he could blame the murder on the captain, but Oscar knew it wouldn't fly. Either way, the hired killer couldn't go through with it. Now they knew that I was capable of accepting Gaylord's money to murder one or both of them.

No. They would have shot me before I had a chance to show a weapon. But that was before this flap.

"Both of you, put on your goddamned jockey shorts so I don't have to look at your ratty junk." I pointed at the empty helm seat. "Oscar, pick up your clothes and put them right there. Now pick up Hovatter's and put them over on this side. Feel anything heavy in there?"

"I do," said Oscar Raney.

"Will I find something heavy in your clothing?"

"Just my fish knife."

"I reached into a small stowage bin, pulled out one of the dock lines and handed it to Oscar. "Tie him up," I said, "then lash him to that cabin-top winch."

I left the helm long enough to grab the shorts that held Hovatter's gun. Against my better judgment, I sniffed the piece of clothing, the pocket that held the pistol. I caught an acrid whiff of spent gunpowder.

Moss couldn't go through with it. Had he shot the bulkhead instead of Oscar?

"Really? Tie him up?" said Oscar.

"Is that too complicated a command?" I said. "Incapacitate the bastard. Make sure he can't screw with us or the boat. Make him kneel before you start because he'll try to fight back. I'll keep this gun pointed right at his belly."

~~~

The morning sail across the bumpy Stream went as well as I could have hoped. No problems with equipment, and we kept Hovatter covered with a wet jib so he wouldn't fry in the sun. By early afternoon, even with the onboard pre-dawn bullshit, we were ahead of the thirty-six-hour schedule I had plotted for arrival at Big Game Club on North Bimini. I had plenty of daylight left to divert to Bimini Sands Resort on South Bimini. If I could charm the dockmaster into letting me poach a slip for an hour or two, I might be able to clear customs and immigration with agents from the airport, plus defuse a couple potential issues.

My first approach to Bimini Sands was no sweat during the day. Charm, however, did not work. Unless we intended to register at the hotel and pay standard dockage fees, we would have to cast off immediately. Also, I was told that a constable had been summoned in regard to the rope-bound, half-naked man in the cockpit.

My cleverness had outpaced my common sense.

Blame lack of sleep.

One last chance. I asked Oscar Raney to produce the oven-ready fish that Lou and Trish had given us back in Key West.

Fish worked fine. Three cold yellowtail in three Ziploc bags. One for the dockmaster, one for the Bahamas Customs representative, an emotion-free nice guy, and one for the constable. He didn't quibble when I pointed out the hole in the hull and asked him to arrest Moss Hovatter for mutiny. I handed over the boat documents, our three passports, my weapon and its registry papers. The constable sniffed my gun and shrugged. I gave him Hovatter's knee-length shorts with the pistol in the pocket. This one flunked the sniff test.

"We have a fine, small jail on South Bimini," the constable explained, "but it's full of Cuban refugees. I will use my motorboat to transport Mister Hovatter to the North Bimini Government Offices. It is the pink building across the street from and a short distance north of Big Game. We will be there before you reach your dockage. Please call on me before five o'clock."

The constable departed with Moss, our passports and the boat papers.

The dockmaster also accepted five twenties for his trouble.

I couldn't get underway fast enough.

~~~

Motoring to North Bimini, I said, "He talked you into shooting through the hull."

"He said it would be a stress reliever," said Oscar.

"It was good advice. Did he break the news to you about your girlfriend?"

"Kind of, but, I suspected all along. I came on this trip to show her that I trusted her. Then douchebag Moss made his comment about me being alone for the rest of my life. To me, that confirmed the shit. He also found my peashooter by snooping around in my duffel bag."

The gun was Oscar's. Where was Hovatter's?

"Did you come out and ask him, too?" I said. "What did he say?"

Something like, "Weird that you're on Gaylord's boat, Oscar. He's been juking around with your true love."

"Were you going to shoot Wilson Gaylord on the dock in Bimini?"

"You bet," said Oscar. "Hovatter talked me into damaging fiberglass instead. He said all women are crazy, anyway. I could take it out on the man's precious boat and not spend the rest of my life in prison." Oscar shook his head, walked to the bow, and spent about four minutes studying the bay water passing us by. When he returned to the cockpit, he said, "Moss wouldn't have gotten down on his knees if he wasn't guilty of something."

"He made sure you had gunpowder residue all over your clothing. If anyone had been hurt on the boat, the bad ju-ju was on you."

"Gotcha. He might have meant to hurt me after all."

"Gaylord might be waiting on the dock over here. Do I need to drop anchor in the harbor until you chill?"

"No, I'm cool."

"How did Moss happen to have your gun in the pocket of his shorts, Oscar?"

Raney shook his head. "I think it was insurance against me doing something dumb."

"Go below now and stay there for the first ten minutes we're at the dock."

"Aye, aye, captain. Okay if a catch a nap?"

"You deserve it."

~~~

Sprinkling rain welcomed me to North Bimini.

I nosed into a vacant slip on the north pier, tossed the dock lines to a marina employee then made one last check in the captain's cabin. Oh, Oscar, you bad boy. The packet that I had put under my skinny mattress was gone. The envelope that once had held four thousand but, when stolen, held thirty-eight twenties packed between two hundred-dollar bills. It hadn't been in Hovatter's shorts, that was for sure.

I felt the cell phone buzz in my pocket before I stepped off the sailboat. The text message saved me from surprise when I walked down the dock to be greeted by Wilson Gaylord and two Scenes of Crime Officers from the Royal Bahamian Police Force. It also told me that Lou Combs had secured the services of a Nassau-based attorney, and Moss Hovatter would be willing to testify against Wilson Gaylord.

Gaylord greeted me coldly. Then, too quickly, noticed the hole in the hull. He demanded to know the whereabouts of Moss Hovatter.

I said, "Mr. Hovatter had to make an exit."

"Where's Oscar Raney?"

"I don't see him, do you?"

He turned to the police officers. "I want Brady Dolan arrested on suspicion of two murders."

"Let's get on with it," I said to the officers. "Please separate me from my accuser right now. Get me into that police van and away from here."

One of them obliged by handcuffing me, shoving me toward the path that led to the main road. A stunning young woman approached, then passed us. I heard Oscar's voice from back near the boat.

"Hey, baby. What are you doing here?"

Shocked, the woman said nothing.

I feared for her life. "Honey," I said, "your timing sucks."

Oscar stepped onto the dock, pulled a gun from under his shirt, and shot a bullet into Wilson Gaylord's chin. It blew off the back of his head. Oscar threw the gun into the salt water and gave himself up to the Bahamian cops.

Lou Combs and I had calculated four or five ways this mess could play out, but this was not a scene we had envisioned.

~~~

As Lou assured me they would, the Bahamians refused entry to the yacht *Swizzle Stick III.* So that I could travel elsewhere, they issued an official document that named me "Master of the Vessel." Even though Wilson Gaylord had presented copies of papers giving Moss Hovatter permission to sail the boat to Bimini, with or without crew, they also refused to prosecute Moss, which worked fine with me. I needed the man's help on the trip to Turks and Caicos. I would compensate him and fly him home before I sold the boat, then wait a few days before returning to Key West to split the proceeds with the two people who had saved my life.

Lou and Trish spent their down payment, the four grand, on an extravagant seaside vacation in Portugal.

The cotton-candy girlfriend, I have no idea.

~~~

About The Authors

1. Murder In Key West
Michael Haskins

Michael Haskins says, "I grew up in North Quincy, Massachusetts, and went through the public school system. I wasn't a student who stood out. If my English teacher in the ninth grade had not told me to put down a copy of Hemingway's short stories (I had taken it off a bookrack during study class) because I was 'too stupid to understand it,' I might never have wanted to read. Thank you Mr. Carlin! In my senior year, I talked my creative writing teacher, Mrs. Shapiro, into getting the school to allow us to publish a creative writing magazine, Counterpoint. Mr. Carlin barely passed me, Mrs. Shapiro gave me A's! Go figure!"

2. A Lucky Man
Jonathan Woods

Jonathan Woods is the author of five pulp noir crime books. His story collection, Bad Juju & Other Tales of Madness and Mayhem ("Hallucinatory, hilarious, imaginative noir."—New York Magazine) was a featured book at the 2010 Texas Book Festival in Austin and won a 2011 Spinetingler Award for Best Crime Short Story Collection. His other books are:

• A Death in Mexico: "Captures that same blend of bleakness and corruption that drives Orson Welles' film noir Touch of Evil."—Booklist;

• Phone Call from Hell and Other Tales of the Damned: "Cleverly written and deeply, often hilariously, twisted."—Booklist;

• Kiss the Devil Good Night: "A frenzied and sprawling masterpiece."—Jon Bassoff; and

• Hog Wild: "Awild glorious ride and a fantastic feast of storytelling...Mixing the gothic with the surreal, the western with pulp."—Ken Bruen.

His stories have appeared in Dallas Noir, Murder in Key West #1 and #2 and other crime fiction anthologies and websites. A former Key West resident, he now divides his time between Dallas and Galveston, Texas.

3. The Itinerary
Roberta Isleib
Writing as Lucy Burdette

Lucy Burdette A/K/A Roberta Isleib is a clinical psychologist and the author of ten mysteries, including *Death In Four Courses*, the second in the Key West food critic series. Her books and stories have been short-listed for Agatha, Anthony, and Macavity awards. She is a past president of Sisters in Crime.

4. Four Fingers and the Dead Drag Queen
Shirrel Rhoades

Shirrel Rhoades is a writer, critic, filmmaker, former college professor, art collector, and publishing consultant. For more than two decades, he and his wife shared their historic classic temple revival style house in Key West with assorted dogs, cats, and a surrogate daughter.

5. Saving Gloria
Jessica Argyle

Jessica Argyle is a writer from Montreal, Canada. She holds an MA from the Creative Writing program of Concordia University and has had many stories published in literary magazines and a collection of short stories (*Arrest Me Before I Write Again*) published in 2011. She is currently at work on a novel-in-progress set in No Name Key.

6. Block
Mike Dennis

After thirty years as a professional musician (piano), Mike Dennis left Key West and moved to Las Vegas to become a professional poker player. He turned to writing when his first novel, *The Take*, was picked up by a publisher in 2009.

His second book, *Setup On Front Street*, was the first of a series of noir novels called *Key West Nocturnes*. These books will lift the veil on Key West and reveal it as a true noir city, on a par with Los Angeles, New Orleans, or Miami.

The Ghosts Of Havana is the second book in that set. The third, *Man-Slaughter*, is now available. The fourth, *The Guns Of Miami*, will be coming in 2013.

In addition, Mike has begun the Jack Barnett / Las Vegas series, centering around a reluctant ex-private investigator in Sin City, USA. The first entry in that series, a novelette called *Temptation Town*, is now available. The second installment, *Hard Cash*, is now available. Mike also has a collection of short stories, *Bloodstains On The Wall*. In addition, his stories have been published in A Twist Of Noir, Mysterical e, Powder Burn Flash, Slow Trains, and *The Wizards Of Words 2009 Anthology*.

In December 2010, Mike moved back to Key West, where he enjoys year-round island living.

7. Ivory Tower
Hal Howland

Hal Howland is the author of *After Jerusalem: A Story and Two Novellas, The Human Drummer: Thoughts on the Life Percussive,* and *Landini Cadence and Other Stories: A Rich Castillo Threesome,* a finalist in the 2011 Next Generation Indie Book Awards and a recipient of the 2012 Eric Hoffer Award for excellence in independent publishing. Several pieces in *The Jazz Buyer* have been nominated for the Lorian Hemingway Short Story Competition and the *Writer's Digest* Popular Fiction Awards. Howland has released three award-winning, critically acclaimed jazz recordings, *The Howland Ensemble, Reiko,* and *10 Years in 5 Days,* and has received a jazz fellowship from the National Endowment for the Arts. Born in Washington, D.C., and raised in Virginia, Europe, and the Middle East, Howland lives in Key West, Florida.

8. Loose Cannons
Tom Corcoran

Tom Corcoran has been a disc jockey, bartender, AAA travel counselor, U. S. Navy officer, screenwriter, freelance photographer, automotive magazine editor, computer graphic artist, and journalist. Corcoran's photographs have appeared on seven Jimmy Buffett album covers. He co-wrote the Buffett hits, "Cuban Crime of Passion" and "Fins." His photos also have appeared on numerous book jackets, including those of Thomas McGuane (*An Outside Chance*), Winston Groom (*Forest Gump*), and Florida novelists Les Standiford (*Black Mountain* and *Last Train to Paradise*, and James W. Hall (*Hot Damn*). Tom's black-and-white photographs of Key West were displayed at the Key West Art and Historical Society's Custom House Museum in 2007.

He is the author of the Alex Rutledge mysteries, including *Gumbo Limbo, Bone Island Mambo, Hawk Channel Chase, The Quick Adiós* (*Times Six*), and others.

Murder in Key West is an annual anthology of short stories by the best mystery writers on the southernmost island. Be sure to look for *Murder in Key West 2* and other exciting mysteries at *AbsolutelyAmazingEbooks.com.*

Please review this book. Reviews help others find *AbsolutelyAmazingEbooks.com* and inspires us to keep bringing you great reading!

Thank you for reading.
Please review this book. Reviews
help others find Absolutely Amazing eBooks and
inspire us to keep providing these marvelous tales.
If you would like to be put on our email list
to receive updates on new releases,
contests, and promotions, please go to
AbsolutelyAmazingEbooks.com and sign up.

For sales, editorial information, subsidiary rights information
or a catalog, please write or phone or e-mail
AbsolutelyAmazingEbooks
Manhanset House
Shelter Island Hts., New York 11965-0342, US
Tel: 212-427-7139
www.AbsolutelyAmazingEbooks.com
bricktower@aol.com
www.IngramContent.com

For sales in the UK and Europe please contact our distributor,
Gazelle Book Services
White Cross Mills
Lancaster, LA1 4XS, UK
Tel: (01524) 68765 Fax: (01524) 63232
email: jacky@gazellebooks.co.uk

www.ingramcontent.com/pod-product-compliance
Lightning Source LLC
Chambersburg PA
CBHW071222260626

47162CB00004B/1394